BEETLE BOY

margaret
willey

carolrhoda LAB
MINNEAPOLIS

Carolrhoda Lab™ is a trademark of Lerner Publishing Group, Inc.

Carolrhoda Lab™
An imprint of Carolrhoda Books
A division of Lerner Publishing Group, Inc.
241 First Avenue North
Minneapolis, MN 55401 U.S.A.

For reading levels and more information, look up this title
at www.lernerbooks.com.

Cover and interior designs © Laura Otto Rinne

Main body text set in Janson Text LT Std 10/14.
Typeface provided by Linotype AG.

Library of Congress Cataloging-in-Publication Data

Willey, Margaret.
    Beetle Boy / by Margaret Willey.
        pages   cm.
    Summary: Terrible memories resurface when Charlie's girlfriend asks
    questions about his childhood.
        ISBN 978–1–4677–2639–9 (trade hard cover : alk. paper)
        ISBN 978–1–4677–4626–7 (eBook)
        [1. Emotional problems—Fiction. 2. Family problems—Fiction.
    3. Dating (Social customs)—Fiction.] I. Title.
    PZ7.W65548Be 2014
        [Fic]—dc23   2013036853

Manufactured in the United States of America
1 – BP – 7/15/14

For Richard Joanisse

"A dreaming
man is a
haunted man."

—Stephen
Vincent Benét

ONE

I am hanging by my fingers out of an open window in the bedroom I once shared with my little brother. There is a horrifying distance between my dangling feet and the dark street below. I want to cry for help, but I don't want to wake up my dad; he hates being woken up; he'll be furious. Instead, I call pleadingly to my brother. *"Li-am! Li-am!"*

The name becomes its own soft scream.

I strain my neck to see what is happening inside my room. I see a thin shadow appear on the water-stained wall, followed closely by a long black rod. Oh God. A gigantic insect has come into my room; it is moving across the floor to the window. I hear the clicking of its claws on the linoleum floor and another sound—a kind of whirring, menacing sound, although its wings are still. One of the beetle's legs is longer than the other five; this is the leg that probes its way to the windowsill as I watch helplessly. Then I see the dark underside of the beetle at the window; it is standing up like a bear; I see its fuzzy, segmented abdomen and where the lower legs are connected to the thorax. The longest leg comes slowly out the window, spiked with coarse hair, the shiny claw passing my hands and my head and still descending—down and down it comes, and the whirring grows louder—until the claw is poised beside my dangling leg. The right leg. It grabs me there, just above the heel of my foot, and the pain is dull but inescapable. I can't get away. I am begging now, crying louder to my brother to help me. "Liam!"

Charlie, you're dreaming again. Wake up! Wake up!

I am awake, struggling to sit up, waving my arms, stuck on my back in the middle of the mattress. Clara has rushed from her bedroom into the living room, where I sleep on her sleeper sofa. She sits on one of the bottom corners of the tangled bed and puts a comforting hand on my good leg. The other leg is in a cast, and it is throbbing.

Another nightmare, Charlie?

"It's the meds," I groan. "Sorry I woke you up again."

You were calling your brother's name. I heard you say "Liam." Your voice sounded like you were strangling.

"God. Sorry."

Liam was in your dream?

"No. No, I was . . . I was just calling him."

Were you looking for him?

"No. No. It wasn't . . . no. It was hallucinatory, Clara. Can you reach the Percodan for me please?"

Which she does, frowning. Then hands me a glass of water.

My girlfriend has made a little invalid station for me beside the sleeper sofa. On the side table there is a lamp with a clicker I can reach easily if I want to stare at the walls; a clock so I can see what hour of the night I'm still awake at; a full glass of water; Tylenol; and the prescription bottle of my new friend, Percodan.

Clara watches me swallow the pill and drink the water. She crosses her bare legs. She takes the glass, sets it on the bedside, still frowning. She is beginning to suspect that something is very wrong inside my head, even though I keep insisting it's the meds. The nights are getting worse, and I often wake her without meaning to. How can she stand it? I lie back and close my eyes and pretend to be falling back to sleep.

Everything okay now, Charlie?

I make a humming sound. Soon I hear her pad away. I promise myself I won't wake her up again. I lay awake for hours. The pain fades and then comes back again around 3 a.m., but I don't call for her. I won't wake her. I let her sleep.

◆ ◆ ◆

In the morning, she wants to hear more about the Liam dream. It surprised her that I would cry out for a brother I never talk about. She is calling out questions to me from the kitchen, where she is making eggs and bacon for me before she heads off to the Rite Aid. She's a pharmacist's assistant. She wears a lab coat and a badge. She has a long shift today; I will be alone for many hours in her tiny house, a house that is the perfect size for her but challenging for me with my crutches, my cast, and my haunted nights.

I just don't get it, Charlie. I mean, you hardly ever say a word about your brother. You say there's nothing to say, but then I hear you screaming his name in the middle of the night!

The kitchen has a wide entryway, and I can see her at the stove from where I am still on my back, propped up with pillows. "I wasn't screaming," I say. "Don't exaggerate." She leans back from the stove so that I can more clearly see her face, and she gives me a look that says she knows she wasn't exaggerating.

"You'll be late for work if you don't move it," I point out, and it's true. She brings a plate of eggs to the bedside table and crosses the room to where her bedroom is. At night, after I am settled in, she sleeps by herself in a double bed from her childhood with a padded white headboard with rainbow peace decals on it. I can't see her dressing, but I hear her; she is rushing, hangers are scraping, clothes are flying, and I am overcome with guilt. What a wreck of a boyfriend I am, literally. When she comes back into the living room, the hub of her house, she is dressed in a red blouse with puffy sleeves and black pants and her hair is piled on top of her head with one of those gigantic plastic clips. I think she is coming over to kiss me good-bye, and I feel a rush of lust for her, lust and remorse, but she doesn't kiss me. Instead, she takes the empty plate from my lap, puts it back on the bedside table, and sits down beside me, straight-backed, all business now.

I know I've asked you this before, but could you please just explain again why you're not in contact with anyone in your family?

"Clara, I don't want to make you late for work."

It is now five minutes past when she usually leaves. She grimaces in frustration at the bedside clock.

Okay, but do you promise we'll talk about this later, Charlie?

I promise we will. My current life is a series of promises, postponements, and escalating nightmares. *Just leave*, I'm thinking. But then she kisses me good-bye with her lips warm and slightly minty and suddenly I don't want her to leave.

I can't explain my nightmares to her. Just like I can't explain what's happening inside my head when I'm awake. I have functioned for over a year without explaining anything important to anyone. But my girlfriend sees herself as a scientist. She collects facts. She requires backstory. She needs to know who and what she's dealing with. She is forming hypotheses and getting worried.

This is the downside of having a girlfriend who apparently, unbelievably, loves me.

◆ ◆ ◆

My answers to her questions about my parents have always been vague. Vague excuses for the early disappearance of my mother, vague explanations for the more recent disappearance of my father, vague references to how it affected me, bored expressions when I am talking about my dad, glassy expressions while I am talking about my mom. Clara especially wants to hear about Mom. Mom got depressed; Mom got sick; Mom needed a different climate for her asthma; Mom knew she wouldn't get custody—all of these things were true, but the real truth is, I had no satisfactory explanation for why Mom left us with Dad long ago. No matter what kind of shape she was in at the time. Not after the kind of mother she had been. How could she have lived without us? How could she spend even one day without seeing us? Playing hide-and-seek with us? Making our oatmeal? Telling us stories?

And knowing that we would be stuck with only Dad—how could she have left us, knowing that? She knew better than anyone that he would be a terrible parent. How could she have not stood outside the window of our crappy new bachelor apartment and just *howled* for us?

◆ ◆ ◆

"It was a long time ago," I finally tell Clara. "My memories are fuzzy." I will myself to sound authoritative.

But I am on crutches in her apartment and I've lost fifteen pounds and I take pain meds all day and have nightmares all night. I am two and a half years younger than she is, and so she sees herself as more wise about family life. She isn't buying my excuses anymore. She gives me one of her we'll-talk-later looks. Then she is gone.

TWO

I am in the twin bed in Mrs. M.'s little basement room, and there is something very, very large moving its body around inside the closet where I keep my belongings. I hear scraping, dragging sounds against the cement walls of the closet. The door is shut, but the scraping sounds stop and shift to the door and then to the doorknob. Whatever is inside the closet is fumbling with the knob, trying to turn it, wanting to come out. I am frozen on the bed, unable to move, afraid to make a sound. Afraid to yell for Mrs. M. The knob on the closet door begins to creakily turn. The door opens a crack, the whirring sound pours out, the room darkens, the crack widens, and there it is, there it is—the black rod, the hairy leg, probing its way out of the closet and into my room. It is coming toward my bed. The claw opens and shuts as it nears me. I manage to sit up, and I find my voice and croak for Mrs. M. "Mrs. Emmmmmmmm."

My own voice wakes me. I am sitting upright on the sleeper sofa, covered in sweat. I made hardly any noise this time. There is no sound from Clara's bedroom. Good, there won't be any questions about Mrs. M., who she was, why I was calling *her*. I look at the clock—it's 3 a.m., and I see that beside the clock,

Clara has left a single Percodan for easier access, next to the glass of water. Thank you, Clara. I take the pill.

But a memory comes to me before the meds pull me under. We are in the alley behind Mrs. M.'s house. We are burning my beetle costume in a metal trash can. We are laughing, making a racket. All of a sudden, Mrs. M. pulls her red wig off of her head and throws it right into the can—the wig is mostly plastic, and it makes a poof of black smoke before it melts into the flames.

◆ ◆ ◆

Somebody was laughing in his sleep last night. That was a nice change.

So I woke her up after all. I am disappointed, but she is smiling, genuinely glad that I was having fun in my sleep. Her smile changes, becomes determined. She is going to pile on some questions now. I brace for them, keeping my expression blank.

Charlie, if your mom moved away before you wrote your books, does that mean she never got to see one of your Beetle Boy performances?

Never. Never. Never. She never even knew I was Beetle Boy. I wouldn't have wanted her to see me in that costume; I would have been so ashamed. She never saw what I did with her stories after she left; she didn't know. I don't tell Clara any of this. I say matter-of-factly, "Nah, she was long gone by then."

Well . . . I think she would have been very proud of you, Charlie. I still remember that time you came to my school. Even then, I noticed how cute you were.

She is tickling me as she says this. She doesn't know that the school visits I did in my own hometown were by far the most excruciating. Just utterly humiliating. Five years. Five terrible years. I performed all over the greater Grand Rapids area as the World's Youngest Published Author—a gigantic storytelling bug. My dad routinely drove over the speed limit to get me from one school to the next, as many as we could manage in one day—sometimes four schools. At first the money poured in. We were flooded with personal checks with names I recognized—the parents of my friends, friends I didn't have anymore because I was too busy being the world's youngest published author. Dad would put the checks and the cash into lunch bags in the trunk of the car and take them to the bank once a week. He was the happy one then; he was on the upswing.

What's wrong, Charlie? You look sick all of a sudden. Is your leg bothering you?

I tell her no. My leg is not bothering me. I took a pill with breakfast; it will send me back to bed once she leaves for work. I will sleep long into the afternoon, hopefully with no dreams.

◆◆◆

Now we are snuggled up on the sleeper sofa together, watching *The Daily Show*, and Clara is wearing one of my thin, faded T-shirts. It kills me when she wears my shirts. They fit her like a boxy dress because she's so tiny. They make it easy to reach her hips and her curvy butt. I slide my hand under the raggedy hem. She makes my kiss into something more, something she will need to pull away from if she really wants to watch Jon Stewart. She doesn't pull away.

Mmmm . . . are you my Beetle Boy?

I am the one who pulls away. My throat is suddenly dry as ash. "Don't call me that, Clara."

Okay, okay, Grouchy. Come back here.

"No, seriously," I tell her, for once not hiding my urgency. "Please, don't ever, *ever* call me that."

(Big sigh) Sometimes I don't understand you, Charlie. You were a child prodigy. You wrote actual books! People bought them! You were famous before you were ten! If it was me, I'd be so proud of that.

I can't continue this conversation. I want her to know me better, but there is so much I can't reveal. So I kiss her again and hope that she'll remember not to call me what I have just asked her not to call me. If she does it again, I might have to kick her off my sleeper sofa. I might have to move out. I just might have to move out. Not that I would have anywhere else in the entire world to go.

◆ ◆ ◆

The fact is that I am pinned like a bug in Clara's living room, caught fast in a cast to my knee. Clara adds to my claustrophobia because she quickly wants to know everything there is to know about me. She asks me question after question. She thinks of different ways to ask the same question. She studies me with scientific curiosity. She probably knows me better than anyone else alive in the world right now, but she doesn't know me at all.

Have I mentioned that I ruptured my Achilles tendon? A

freak accident, and I do not use the term *freak* lightly. For three weeks I have been in this cast, walking on crutches, slowly recovering. Before that I lived in a downtown motel offering weekly rentals and no questions. Before that I lived with Mrs. M., but I had to move out when she left to go live with her sister. Before that I lived with Dad and Liam on Grove Street. I'm quite the nomad.

Clara's house is a one-story bungalow with a tiny attached garage; there are no stairs, very convenient for a cripple. Her parents own the house, and they charge her very low rent so that she can pay off her student loans from her associate's degree in pharmacy tech. So I am living off Clara's parents, which was never my plan, but oh well. I accepted Clara's rescue of me as I accepted Mrs. M.'s rescue of me, although with Mrs. M. it was my choice. Clara's rescue was more of a total surrender to my brokenness and to her own willingness to collect me.

So here I am. By day I am mostly sitting up on the sleeper sofa, watching Clara's TV. By night I sleep and wake up and sleep, always on my back. I can walk around the house a little bit on my crutches, but it's a bad tear and I am generally not supposed to put any weight on my right leg. When I move through the rooms, of which there are basically four besides the living room, it takes me forever. My life has slowed to a terrible crawl.

Clara is watching me eat dinner—soup and tuna melts— forming her next question. Please don't ask me anything about the books, Clara; don't make me go there, not the books, anything but the books. Don't make the titles come into my consciousness. Too late, too late! *Meet Beetle Boy. Beetle Boy Crawls Again. Beetle Boy and the Lonely Spider. Beetle Boy and the Mean*

Ladybug. The titles appear in my mind, bright red and off-center, like a little kid scribbled them, because a little kid did scribble them. The title fonts are my own wimpy handwriting. I am suddenly gagging on my tuna melt.

Are you in pain? Is it time for a pill?

"No more pills. I think I need to go outside. Just for a few minutes."

Charlie, the doctor said . . .

"I don't care what she said. I need some fresh air. Just get the crutches, okay? Please? The moon is out. Let's go outside, just for a minute."

Hold on, Charlie, I'll get you a sweater too.

She is so helpful! Why isn't she sick of me? She never complains. Maybe she thinks I'm actually getting better. She doesn't know I'm cracking up. She asks me the most innocent questions: "Why won't you just call your brother? Why hasn't your mom tried to get in touch with you?"

It's a warm April night with a full moon. We walk around the block in the moonlight.

What happened to all those cute books you wrote, Charlie? You saved some of them, right?

I grimace, not so much because I am in pain but because I want her to see that all I can manage at the moment is walking.

We make it all the way around—four blocks of walking on crutches, the most exercise I've had since the accident. Clara says she is proud of me. I am hoping the walk will help me to sleep better. But another dream awaits me. This one is more absurd than scary, naturally, because it involves my dad.

A commotion from outside has awakened me, and I crawl on all fours, dragging my leg, scraping it on Clara's wood floors, making my way to the picture window in the living room. I pull the blinds up a few inches and lift my head to the sill, resting my chin on it to brace myself for whatever I will see. There, in the street in front of the house, is my dad, riding a black horse, wearing a cowboy hat and a fringed leather vest. He is shouting at the moon, and his horse is bucking and making a tremendous clatter with its hooves. Oh, wait. It's not a horse. It has six legs, and its hooves are claws. Dad is sitting in a saddle on its flat, shiny back. Dad sees my face in the window.

"Charlie!" he hollers, and the beetle also screams in recognition—an alien sound, like brakes screeching. "We know you're hiding in there!"

I pull back from the window, appalled that they have found me. I am crouched on the floor under the window, shaking and holding my ears. Dad is laughing his insane, bellowing laugh, his drunken laugh. The beetle screams.

I wake up in my bed and take a pill.

THREE

How did I find someone like Clara? A normal girl who says she loves me. And why does she love me? Is love different for her, something you can just extend, like a handshake, to another person? *Hello, I'm Clara. I have love available—here, take some.*

The first time she said she loved me we were walking away from downtown, where we had just had lunch, my treat. I was living in the motel then, working at the bike shop, and I had a little extra money because the motel was so cheap. I was a high school graduate (barely) and I was single and I had money in my wallet. And I would have taken Clara out to lunch every single day, just to be able to sit across a table from her and watch her chew. I had never met a girl who seemed to enjoy just being with me. She laughed at my jokes. She said I had irresistible eyes.

Clara is tiny, but that day she walked beside me and kept pace with me, scurrying a little on the icy sidewalks. I was on my way back to the bike shop, which was a block away from the Rite Aid. She gave this big, happy sigh and tipped her head back and looked at the sky and said, "I think I might be falling in love with somebody named Charlie."

I did not stop walking, but we had been chatting about something else and I know I stopped talking. For several beats.

"Oops, that just popped out of me," she said. "I can take it back."

"What do you mean, you can take it back?" I asked, confused. Was she kidding about it?

"I mean I can take it back if you didn't like hearing it." She was getting nervous now; she giggles when she's nervous.

"It's just that . . . Clara, how can you like me that much . . . already?"

We had come to a full stop. She was looking up at me, shivering and squinting in the bright winter sun. "You like me already, don't you?"

"Yeah, but . . . you're *beautiful*."

"Well, you're pretty cute, Charlie. But that isn't the only reason."

"You think I'm *cute*?"

Clara exhaled noisily, then put an arm around my waist and started us both walking again, picking up the pace. "We'd better keep moving if I'm going to get back to work on time."

We walked a few more blocks to the Rite Aid, talking about her job and my job, like nothing had changed or like it was totally possible that a beautiful girl was falling in love with me. When actually I was in a state of shock about it that has never completely gone away. When we came to the sliding glass doors of the Rite Aid, she said, "Call me tonight?"

It was very convenient, the way she would instruct me to

call her, so that it never seemed like I was calling her because I couldn't stop myself from calling her.

But love? How do you love someone when you are carrying around as much secret baggage as I am carrying around? How do you go from that to intelligently, generously loving another person? I have no idea.

◆ ◆ ◆

Okay, let me get this straight, Charlie. Your mom ran away when you were seven. And after that you lived with your dad in a little apartment over on Grove Street, right?

"Didn't we already talk about this today, Clara?"

I was just wondering where you lived before your mom left. What happened to your house?

Clara, in her innocence, believes that every family lives in a house. I take a sip of the coffee she has just brought me, stalling. How much to tell her? How deep to go into it? How awful to remember that place, that apartment.

"My memories are pretty fuzzy," I try for the millionth time.

Oh, but they are such unfuzzy memories. Painfully sharp, actually. We moved into the apartment in the middle of a blizzard, a snowstorm from hell, Liam crying, snot running all down the front of his snowsuit. I remember telling him to shut up. Like, over and over. I feel terrible about that now, but I was dying inside for Dad. It's so strange to think of this now, but I was worried sick about him after Mom left. Like Liam was irrelevant on the scale of tragedy. I felt this way for years. Dad was the eye of the storm, and Liam was just a little branch blown off a tree. No wonder he hates me.

I meet Clara's eyes and confess, "There was never a house for the Porter family. We never got our act together enough to have a house. We always lived in crappy apartments."

Her face falls. I ask her if she could make me a quick sandwich in the kitchen. I want her in a different room than the room I am in, a room that now contains a terrible memory, one that she has caused to surface.

◆ ◆ ◆

The complex was named Green Grove Apartments, and ours was No. 6. The three-story building was so dilapidated and unsafe that it was condemned and torn down less than a year after we left the premises. There are no longer any traces of it; the corner where I spent most of my childhood has been converted to a strip mall with half a dozen little businesses—shoe repair, Thai restaurant, chiropractor. All of this could have made the No. 6 apartment easier to forget, but from where I sit in Clara's house, the rooms are calling back to me—all three and a half of them—the main room with a kitchen along one wall, the little one-window bedroom I shared with Liam, Dad's master bedroom, and a bathroom the size of a closet with a rotten floor and a rust-stained toilet and a shower stall so small I don't know how Dad even got himself in there. Liam was afraid to take a shower—he washed himself at the sink for all those years, standing on a towel. Somehow all three of us went from those first traumatic days of realizing this was our new home without Mom to feeling like we would live there forever. Then, over the course of a single year, we were all relocated, and the building was gone. Did it ever exist?

Dad's car. An old Toyota hatchback. Silver. January. Dad telling us this was going to be the coolest apartment ever for the three amigos, the three dudes, with plenty of space for entertaining (no furniture, except for one sofa and three beds), no bedtime rules (we all had insomnia), and no women allowed (this lasted about two weeks). Eventually, we had furniture— beds, bedding, a television, dishes, and used appliances—but for those first few days, it was like we had crash-landed into an empty bunker. We were scared. Have I mentioned Liam crying? That wasn't the worst of it.

Dad bought all these groceries for us right away—all the forbidden food that Mom wouldn't let us eat—ice-cream pies, pizza rolls, Pop-Tarts, Coke. He carried these supplies into the bachelor pad, a bag in each arm. But that was when we learned that the ancient refrigerator didn't work—it was plugged in and turned on but dead as a doornail, and it smelled really bad when we opened the door. It smelled like death. And it was like the third thing in the apartment that wasn't working. My dad put the grocery bags on the floor, and then he did this thing that I'd never seen him do before—he balled his hands up into two fists and he put his fists into his eye sockets and then he just let out this really, really, really weird noise and then he yelled my mom's name in this insanely high voice. *Lucinda!* He yelled *Lucinda* three times, like the broken refrigerator was her fault. Then he put his arms around his head and started quaking. And making sounds. And my dad was not someone who made those sounds.

I moved to his side, tugged on the hem of his sweatshirt, and said, manfully, "Hey, come on over here in our new living room and lie down on this nice, comfortable sofa, Dad. Take a load off."

"Take a load off" was one of his own expressions. I tugged harder, and Dad let me lead him to the sofa with his arms still wrapped around his head. He lowered himself onto the lumpy sofa and lay on his side, still making those sounds. They terrified me, but I made my voice especially cheery.

"This is a great place," I said. "Wow, we can really be the three amigos here. Relax, Dad. How 'bout I tell you a little story?"

Because Mom used to do that. Mom always said that a "little story" was a present to make you feel safe. To help you sleep. I came closer to my dad's head and began telling him one of my favorites. This one was about a character that just happened to be a beetle. A happy beetle with very poor eyesight, which made it necessary for him to wear glasses. I remembered the story vividly, although it had been a long time since I'd heard it last. I used the voice that she had used when she was trying to soothe us into sleep—kind of hushed, kind of excited, and I did this thing with my hands—the same thing she did—lifting them up and then bringing them back down, sometimes clasping them when I paused for emphasis.

My dad's shoulders stopped shaking, and he uncovered his head. He was lying very still. If I hadn't noticed that his eyes were open, I might have thought that I had lulled him to sleep. I got halfway through the story, and then I stopped. Dad blinked at me, focusing intently. His eyes were a little wet, a little bloodshot, but other than that he looked perfectly normal.

"Go on," he said.

"You like it?"

"Go on," he repeated. "Finish the story."

I kept going—details about the beetle were coming back

to me with total clarity, almost faster than I could speak them. Dad sat up and rearranged himself on the sofa, leaning forward now, hands on his knees but keeping very still, listening to every word, watching me without moving, the way a cat watches a—yes—beetle, before it pounces.

"The end," I said. I exhaled noisily. I was drained. I sat down on the couch beside him and covered my head as he had done earlier. Dad pushed my arms away and ruffled my hair. When he spoke, his voice was raspy and excited.

"I want you to write it down. Just like you told me there, write that story down. Here, I'll get you a piece of paper." He got up from the sofa and rummaged in a box on the kitchen counter for a couple of old utility bills, still sealed in their envelopes. "Write what you just told me," he said, handing me the envelopes and a pen. I wanted to tell him that I had just told him one of Mom's bedtime stories, which he wouldn't have known about since he was never around at our bedtime, but we had a deal—the three amigos—no talking about Mom. Liam wasn't so good at it yet, but I was totally cooperating.

"That was a damn good story, Charlie," he said. "If you think of another one, write it down too."

"There's lots more stories about the beetle," I said. "He gets friends. And he tries living in a tree." I was trying to indirectly tell him that the stories weren't actually mine.

"We're on to something," he said. "I don't think most seven-year-olds could come up with a story that good."

"Well . . . if you want to know the truth . . ."

"Start writing," he said. "Don't talk, *write*!"

I wrote as best I could in my scribbly handwriting. I probably misspelled every other word, but I put my heart into it for

Dad. He was unloading the groceries onto the kitchen counter as I wrote.

"Keep writing, Charlie-boy," he said. "I'll go get us some ice to keep the food cold till tomorrow." He put his coat back on, whistling. Before he left, he checked on Liam, who had cried himself to sleep on a bare mattress in our soon-to-be new bedroom. This seemed like a hopeful sign to me—Dad was still our dad. He would handle the situation.

I had successfully revived him.

I got it into my head that Mom's story had saved him and, by saving him, saved me. That was incorrect. That was an early big mistake.

FOUR

I am in the little corner grocery store where I used to buy cereal, milk, and junk food whenever Dad left money for us in the food jar. I am at the checkout counter, getting ready to pay for a box of frozen waffles, when I hear Liam yelling my name from outside the store. I leave my waffles on the counter and go back to the glass door, where I see that four-year-old Liam has followed me from our apartment, and he is standing naked in the middle of the parking lot. Behind a parked car, very near my naked brother, I see several hairy black legs showing; something is crouched behind the car, hiding. I rush back to the counter to pay for my food so I can save my brother, but all I have in my pockets are ripped-out pages from assorted Beetle Boy books. No money! The clerk says I have to put all the food back, which takes forever. When I finally make it back out to the parking lot, Liam is gone. Where is he? Where is the beetle? Behind the car—no beetle, no Liam—nothing but a pile of bones and more torn-out pages. Liam! Liam!

Charlie! Charlie! Stop rolling around! You're going to hurt yourself!

"Oh . . . what? Oh, okay. Okay. I'll just go back to sleep.

You were calling for your brother again. Why were you doing that? What was going on in your dream?

"I told you, you can't ask me to explain my dreams. I promise I'll sleep now, okay? Thanks for checking on me."

I turn away from her and thump my pillow. Make a big show of returning to peaceful sleep. She sits at the side of the mattress for a long time.

◆ ◆ ◆

Her parents want to meet me, which is only fair, since I have been camping out in their daughter's living room for weeks, the same daughter who waits on me hand and foot whenever she's home. "Tell me what they know," I say. "So I can prepare."

Well . . . they do know that you're my boyfriend, Charlie.

"Oh God."

No, they're glad I have a new boyfriend! They didn't like my old boyfriend. And they totally get that somebody has to help you recover from your accident. I mean . . . since your parents can't. So it makes sense to them that you're staying here.

"Do they know you've seen me naked?"

Well . . . that's pretty obvious, isn't it?

"Do they know that I've seen *you* naked?"

(Laughs) We didn't discuss it! They probably think you can't do anything because of your broken leg.

Which is only partly true. Every few days we try to have sex, but so far, it is the worst combination of pain and pleasure you can possibly imagine. Where afterward you are trying for like five minutes not to scream. Then, a few days later, it starts seeming like a good idea again.

These efforts only happen in Clara's bed. Somehow the sofa—my recovery station and the site of my nightmares— seems a terrible place to be romantic or even energetic. Not that Clara's bed is the greatest place for sex. Sometimes it seems like we are having sex at a party in the room of some little kid. But she uses the headboard to brace herself gently on top of me. I have to lie on my back, naturally. It's very limiting, but it has its rewards.

◆ ◆ ◆

I find the fact that Clara is an older woman exciting, although neither of us knew much of anything about sex when we met. Apparently, her previous boyfriend was very conflicted about having sex before marriage; they only tried it a few times. So we were not virgins, but we were morons. Actually, before I tore out my Achilles, we had sex twice—once in her car, *very* moronic, and once on the beach in the moonlight, romantically moronic. I am sure it would have been just as traumatic and humiliating as the few sexcapades from my senior year of high school if it hadn't been for Clara acting like it was perfectly okay for us to be awkward at sex—like maybe it was even better than being experienced—because it was going to be so much fun to improve. Why did she think that? Why was she so optimistic about everything? Is it because she's pretty? She tells me I'm handsome! Sometimes after she says it, I want to run and look into a full-length mirror, to see if something about me has radically changed. I don't know what it would feel like to ever believe in my own handsomeness.

Who besides Clara has ever expressed pleasure about my appearance?

And knowing that she is attracted to me—it's like a superpower, the ability to become worthy of her attention. It's just that right now her attention is so confusingly inescapable! She keeps trying to dissect me! And now—God help me—the parents are coming! I am fucking terrified to meet Clara's parents. I'm not good with parents—parents bring only disaster, humiliation, and pain.

Ugh, I know I have to do it. I have to meet Don and Susan. To earn my spot on the sleeper sofa and keep Clara close to me, helping me, fetching my crutches, rubbing my aching back, bringing me food.

◆◆◆

One month after the three amigos moved into the bachelor apartment, Dad took the first two of the beetle stories to the public library and typed them on a computer. He corrected all the spelling and transcribed my sentences into complete, grammatically correct sentences. Probably a librarian helped him.

After that he contacted his old friend Sam Church, the only person he knew personally who was any sort of artist. Dad offered him half of our eventual book sales if he would illustrate the books. Sam said yes. The next week Sam brought over a used computer and a scanner that had been in a closet where he worked at a downtown copy store. I was home when he arrived, and I watched him come into the living room, grinning ear to ear and making a big fuss about how nice the apartment was. *Are you blind?* I was thinking.

"You did it, Danny-boy," Sam said. He had long hair to his shoulders and a full beard and a raspy laugh. "It sure is good to see you happy again, like the old days."

Even at age six, I knew this was a dig at Mom and I didn't like it. But seeing Dad laughing and popping open beer cans with his friend was surprisingly heartening. Sam was even letting Liam sit on his lap, something Dad never did. And Sam had read both of the first two beetle books, and he was treating me like they were going to change the world. "Oh, you have a rare gift, son," he said to me. "You and your pop are really onto something now."

Can he be right? I wondered.

I looked at Dad. He was beaming proudly, happy to include his friend in our soon-to-be success. I looked at Liam, playing with Sam's beard, singing a little song to himself. I looked around the apartment. Maybe it wasn't so bad. Maybe we were really onto something. Maybe it would be easy and involve no further suffering.

All this time, I was going to a new school, doing my homework, playing with a few new friends from the apartment complex, and taking care of Liam, who was in pre-K and quickly becoming the kindergartner from hell. His teacher kept asking me to have my mother call her, and I kept telling her I would. At one point, she asked me why no one ever answered my home phone. I happened to know that we no longer had a home phone, only Dad's cell phone, whose number I was not supposed to give out. I said, very calmly, "My mom has two jobs so nobody is ever at our house during the day." I was starting to lie routinely.

"Oh really?" Mrs. Dahlia's eyebrows shot up. "Then who takes care of you boys?"

"Our grandmother," I said. "We go to her house after school."

"Do you think your grandmother would be willing to talk to me about Liam's behavior?"

My mind raced for an answer. "She doesn't speak English, ma'am. She's from Spain."

Liam's teacher made a face of bewilderment. "Your father is Spanish?"

"Right," I said. I grabbed Liam's hand and hurried away. When Dad came home, carrying a pizza, I brought up Mrs. Dahlia. "She wants to talk to you about Liam."

"No way. I have no time for wacko teachers."

"She's nice, Dad," I insisted. "Pretty too."

"Pretty?" Dad perked up. "How old would you say?"

"Younger than you. But here's something you should know. I told her you were Spanish."

"Why in the world—"

"She was asking me about Mom. I told her my grand-mother took care of us. My Spanish grandmother."

This made him laugh—a rare accomplishment. "That's a good one, Charlie-boy. Ha-ha. Leave it to me. I'll take care of it." He laughed again and chucked me under the chin. "Qué pasa, Charlie?"

The next morning Dad called the school, speaking with a slight Spanish accent, while Liam and I snickered behind our hands. The office put him straight through to Mrs. Dahlia, and

Dad spoke with a combination of Hispanic charm and fatherly concern and it was a home run with Mrs. Dahlia. He offered to come in that same night and hear her thoughts on Liam. When he hung up, he winked at Liam and said, "You're one lucky amigo, hanging around with Senorita Dahlia."

Liam said, "I hate her."

This surprised even Dad. "Whoa, little amigo, you don't want to talk that way about your first teacher."

"All she ever does is yell at me."

"I'll talk some sense into her," he promised.

Talk some sense into her. It was something he used to say regularly about Mom, and so I wasn't optimistic about Mrs. Dahlia. I looked across the table at Liam. He looked unusually happy, apparently thrilled that Dad was going to talk some sense into his teacher. The strangest things made him happy. I would die before I'd want Dad to visit my teacher.

"Move it, boys, get yourselves ready for school," Dad said. It was Wednesday, his day to meet Sam and critique the latest illustrations. According to Dad, the drawings were "phenomenal," his new favorite word. I had overheard him telling several people on the phone that I was a phenomenal writer. I knew perfectly well that I wasn't a phenomenal writer, but I was hoping against hope that the illustrations would take the book to a new level. And somehow make them seem less stolen.

"When do I get to see the illustrations?" I asked Dad while I threw together two lunches.

"Soon," he promised. "Maybe this weekend. Prepare to be blown away."

◆ ◆ ◆

Clara has been on a cleaning and organizing rampage ever since her parents agreed to come over and have lunch with us and meet me, the invalid moocher boyfriend. I am watching a sitcom after a pizza when I hear Clara poking around in the closet of her bedroom, where I have recently stored my ridiculously small cache of personal belongings. I grab my crutches and hobble into the bedroom, calling her name. "Clara? Clara? What are you doing?"

Just rearranging, Charlie.

She is standing on a stool, moving things around on the topmost shelf of her closet. One of her outstretched hands is touching my boxes. I stand behind her and struggle not to knock the stool out from under her feet with my crutch.

"Could you just leave those alone?" I say.

But Clara has tipped the closest box with her outstretched hand, and it falls from the shelf into her open arms. She pops down from the stool and turns to me, holding it, a cardboard box. A box I kept after Mrs. M. bought me a laptop for high school graduation. The box was heavy and nondescript and had a folding lid. Clara rattles it, her eyes bright with curiosity.

What's in it, Charlie? Anything you might need?

Anything I might need? Yes, a few odd things that I need, although I could never in a million years have explained why. Why do I need photos of people I am unrelated to? Why do I need a gaudy, fake-diamond encrusted pen? Why do I need a card from my only birthday with Mrs. M.—why did I keep that card? Why do I still have a flyer from the first author conference, the day that I met her?

"Could you just put it back for now? Please? And we'll go through it sometime when I'm not so tired?"

She is miffed. She turns her back to me, lifts the box up, reaching mightily and shoving the box back onto the top shelf of her closet. But not before a single wallet-sized photo makes its way under the lid and flutters to the floor. I know whose photo it is without needing to see it—Rita Marie Dean, pretty in a fierce, beady-eyed way, the answer to a desperate six-year-old's prayers.

It's a school photo of a little girl! With red hair. Who is she, Charlie?

My answer is an unimaginative lie. "A cousin who died."

Clara's face droops with concern. Another sad story. I distract her from the closet by asking her if there is anything good in the kitchen for dessert. She follows me into the kitchen to make me something, something to cheer us both after my tragic revelation.

Ice cream? A waffle with chocolate syrup? And you can tell me more about your cousin, okay?

I embellish the lie for half an hour, making up people, places, and events. We have waffles with ice cream, with chocolate syrup and M&M's on top. Clara is trying to help me gain weight. The pain pills have killed my appetite. Clara is quiet, saddened by my fake memories.

You should hear the real ones, I think. I make a mental note to get the box out of her closet and hide it somewhere else ASAP.

FIVE

After the first few terrible months at Green Grove Apartments, I asked Dad to please, please find us a babysitter. He said no way could he afford one, but I happened to know that his father in Jamaica—Grampa Ned—had sent him a big check. A letter had arrived in one of those thin blue envelopes that you can see through with foreign stamps all over it, and when I held it up to the light, I saw that there was a check in it. Then I just had to know how much, so I did this thing I saw Mom do a couple of times, open letters with steam from the teakettle and then close them back up again with a little glue, except Mom would stand at the stove and cry. Me, I was pretty happy. Grampa Ned's check was for $10,000.

"Dad, if you hire somebody young, you hardly have to pay her anything. And with a babysitter, you would be totally free twenty-four-seven to work with Sam on my books."

I wasn't thinking only of Liam. The girl I had already chosen to be our sitter lived in the same apartment building as us. I had decided that I loved her madly. Rita had red braids so tight that she had a bright white part down the back of her head. She was an older woman—almost twelve. I wanted her to be in the same room with me as much as possible. I wanted to impress her with my budding career. I wanted her to sit beside me on our ratty sofa. I wanted to watch her eating day-old pizza at our dirty kitchen table. You get the picture.

Rita became our first post-Mom babysitter. Dad hired her to work from three until six on school days and just about every Friday and Saturday night for the next three months, freeing him up for whatever dates he could arrange in his new bachelor life. He paid her five dollars an hour—what a cheapskate—but I guess she was okay with it.

I worshipped her. Did she like me? Maybe. As much as a twelve-year-old girl can like a geeky six-year-old who talks incessantly about himself. Every so often, she would squeeze her eyes shut and cover her ears and tell me to *pleeeeeassse shut up*! It was adorable.

Unfortunately, she couldn't stand Liam. She ignored his lame attempts to also get her attention, despite that he was a pretty cute kid, much cuter than me—he had inherited Dad's blond good looks, but I surpassed him in charm and sophistication. I knew better than to gurgle and spit milk across the kitchen table or climb to the top of the fridge and sit up there like the Cheshire cat or march out of the bathroom with no pants on, waving his dick. Anything to get her to pay attention to him.

"Watch me dance, Rita!" he would crow. Then he would fling himself around the room, whirling his arms, wearing a cape made from a dish towel. Or he would break into song for no reason, singing whatever ridiculous song he had learned at pre-kindergarten that day in a piping voice, with his face way too close to her face. She would push him away, asking, "What is wrong with you?"

"Seriously, what is wrong with your brother?" she asked me. She had locked him in the bedroom for a time-out while the two of us watched TV in the living room at maximum volume to drown out his hollering.

"Wrong how?" I asked back.

"Is there something about your brother that your dad didn't tell me?"

This gave me pause. "There's nothing wrong with him," I insisted. "He's just a creepy kid."

"He is creepy," she agreed. I had snuck my hand onto her closest arm, and she shook it away. "Stop hanging on me! God! I can't stand that!"

But she was more impatient than angry. She never really got mad at me like she got mad at Liam. I knew the difference. It meant the world to me.

After that conversation, I would sometimes deliberately imitate Liam—his shrill voice, his constant jittery movements. The way he would sometimes run in place while he was speaking. I would do it to make Rita laugh. And she did laugh. We bonded over our contempt for Liam. Did he know? Was he too little to notice? Did it register that I was mocking him to score points with Rita?

Liam. Little Brother. I am so sorry. No wonder you hate me.

◆ ◆ ◆

It would have been so much easier to meet Clara's parents at a chain restaurant—the four of us in our places at a square table, the awkward silences filled by restaurant clatter. But my broken leg prevented this—our meeting had to be in Clara's house, the place where Clara tended to all my needs. Clara had prepared everything, including putting away my pills and folding up the sleeper sofa so that the room looked less like an invalid's hovel.

"How are you, dear?" Clara's mom asks, settling herself beside me on the sofa, a move that makes me feel instantly panicky. But her tone is kind. It is obvious from the first few minutes of the visit that Susan and Don are going to go easy on me. They are nice people—big surprise—but I can tell that they are confused about what to make of Clara's new boyfriend.

"Much better than last week," I say. I am wearing real clothes for the occasion, shorts and my only shirt with a collar. I am already tired.

"How long before you can get out of that cast?" she asks, pointing to it.

I tell her a couple of weeks.

"What will you do then?"

Clara interrupts, tells them about the big plastic boot that is coming next.

"Did you get a leave of absence from your job?" Susan asks.

I tell her yes, although the last thing I care about these days is my stupid job at the bike shop. "I'll go back as soon as I can. I should have a better idea of when after my next doctor's appointment." I am making an effort to sound like I have everything figured out. Susan and Don seem to be buying it. I finish warmly, "I don't know what I would have done without Clara."

"She's a jewel," Susan agrees.

"Clara says you have no family in the area," Don says. "That can't be easy."

This throws me momentarily because Clara knows that I have a mom and a brother living in nearby Grand Rapids, a rather recent development. She pokes her head back into the living room just long enough to give me a private warning look. She probably didn't want to explain the extent of my estrangement from my family. Not to a set of parents who are as involved and adoring as hers are.

"No, it's not easy," I agree, going along with Clara's story. "You think you can make it on your own, and then something like this happens."

Clara—the jewel—comes back into the living room with a tray of cheese and crackers.

While passing it around, she tells her parents that my father lives in Jamaica. I had actually told her this, although it is more of a suspicion than a fact. I was pretty sure he had headed south to hit up his dad permanently, taking his soon-to-be second wife with him. Although it was hard for me to picture him still married after a whole year. But who cares?

"You'll be back on your feet in no time, Charlie," Susan says. "Let us know if there's any way Don or I can help. We're only an hour away, and we're happy to lend a hand—doctor's appointments, groceries, whatever."

Don chimes in: "I'd like to take both of you out for dinner once you're a little more mobile."

"Great," I say. "That sounds great, Mr. Morrison. We'll be sure to keep you posted."

Clara and her mom disappear again into the kitchen, leaving me alone with Don. There is suddenly a thick silence between us, and I flounder in it, trapped. I am afraid to look directly at him. It freaks me out to be alone with a father, anyone's father. I am suddenly soaked in sweat. I wonder if he can smell my fear.

Clara comes back into the room after an eternity with a platter of sandwiches, announcing that we are going to eat lunch in the living room because that's easier for me.

"Fine with me," Don says agreeably.

"Good thinking, sweetie!" exclaims Susan.

Then we are eating the sandwiches, Clara's parents treating her like she is a total genius for having the idea to eat in the living room. It is easy to see why Clara is so positive. Her parents are in awe of her. They must be wondering as they eat what right I have to be under the same roof as her.

Still, they were trying. They leave an hour later, Susan insisting that they don't want to tire me out too much. Like it matters. Like there might be some other project that I will soon begin. When, actually, I am finished for the day.

Clara gives me a big hug when they have driven away.

My mom told me she thinks you're adorable.

"I need a nap," I say, hiding the fact that I am on the verge of total collapse.

Shall I open the sleeper?

But I had already settled myself on the sofa and tipped sideways, sprawling lengthwise end to end. I am seconds from sleep. The minute I let go, my brain helpfully provides me with this:

I know that the beetle has climbed into my father's double bed in the Grove Street apartment; I hear the mattress rustling from my own bedroom. I hear its wings crackle and scrape together as it settles itself down. I am afraid of what will happen when my dad comes home from his date. I know I have to warn him, but I am afraid to leave my room, afraid the beetle will scuttle off Dad's bed and attack me. But I have to try.

So I move fearfully in the dark and find myself at the door of the apartment, where I hear that someone is outside, about to come in. A key turns in the door, and there is Dad—or is it Dad? It is Dad, but he has two beetle claws instead of hands, and in one claw he's holding an open can of Bud and there is lipstick all over his face, and through my fear I manage to warn him in a strangled whisper that there is a big beetle waiting for him in his bed.

"It's not in my bed," Dad says, chuckling. "It's right there behind you, Charlie-boy."

He laughs harder, and the whirring starts up and I cover my eyes, afraid to turn around. Something pokes me, hard, on the back of my right leg. I want to scream, but I don't—I keep the scream silent so that Dad won't hear it. He comes inside, unafraid, and I run past him, out the door into the darkness. I stumble blindly down the metal stairs, leaving him to fend for himself with the beetle that wants his bed.

SIX

Dad never got anywhere with Liam's kindergarten teacher. Apparently, she was a newlywed. She appreciated Dad's willingness to meet her after school, but he came back to the apartment from his meeting telling us that she had "a bone up her ass" and was "too strict," "too picky," and even "prejudiced against boys."

"Did you talk some sense into her?" Liam asked hopefully.

"Try not to piss her off for a few days," Dad instructed. "I don't want to talk to her again. She gave me a headache with all her whining. She did admit that you're smart, Leemster. We both know who you get *that* from."

Later, I approached him while he was grinning at the television and watching his favorite team win—the Oakland Raiders. "Did you find out what's wrong with Liam, Dad?" I asked.

Still smiling, not looking at me. "Nothing wrong with Leemster."

"Dad, he does really weird stuff. You wouldn't believe some of the stuff. Just ask Rita."

Staring at the screen. "Rita's not your babysitter anymore. I'm finding you a new one."

I was devastated. "Dad, she's good. She's the *best*. She helps me with my homework. She does the dishes." Actually, I did the dishes and said it was Rita. I wanted to add: Her hair smells like peaches. Her teeth are perfect. Her fingernail polish blinds me. I finished hopelessly, inaccurately, "She's very fair."

Not that Dad was listening. Apparently one of his new girl-friends had a daughter who needed money, and so Rita was out of the picture. (I saw her a few more times before she and her mother moved away. She told me on the rusted steps of the apartment complex that she didn't like babysitting because she hated little kids. This only increased my love for her.)

The next babysitter was Trudy. Daughter of Melissa, briefly known as Delicious Melicious. Trudy didn't last very long, though, because Delicious didn't last long. Apparently, the last few times Trudy babysat for us, Dad didn't bother to pay her. Her mother left a message on our answering machine, saying it was bad enough that he had cheated on her without also cheating her daughter out of her money. He owed Trudy fifteen dollars.

I was in the kitchen when Dad played this message back. He looked at me, shook his head, and muttered "women." The next day I took fifteen dollars from the food money jar, and I took it to school and made a show of presenting it to Trudy in the hallway outside of her classroom. I told her it was from my dad and that he was sorry. "He's also really sorry about what he did to your mom."

She made a disbelieving face but took the money.

I had become aware of a terrible pattern in Dad's behavior: he changed his mind about women way too fast, sometimes after only one date—a date that he would have gone to all kinds of trouble to arrange. I was also noticing that he spent a lot of our limited budget on impressive first dates at expensive restaurants and dance clubs. It kept us constantly broke, and nobody made him the least bit happy for more than a few weeks.

After the Trudy incident, my dad accepted my role as the babysitter finder. I made sure never to hire anyone with any ties to him. At school, I studied the sixth graders, always on the lookout for a cute girl to make mac and cheese the way I liked it (extra soupy), to stay up late with me on the couch (and not push me away if I wanted to get right up next to her), to let me smell her hair. I hired half a dozen babysitters this way, approaching the girls, asking them if they were interested in a job, even tracking down their phone numbers so that my dad could call the parents if a girl seemed willing.

But they did not last. We were routinely left alone with these girls, sometimes for four or five nights a week. Either my dad found a way to alienate them, mostly by forgetting to pay them or being rude to them when he came home drunk, or maybe the girls themselves found the hours spent with two anemic boys too much to deal with for more than a few months at a stretch. I always turned on the charm with these girls, but no one ever measured up to my memories of Rita, the first girl in the bachelor pad, the first girl who let me be physically close to her. Did I love her more than I love Clara?

I'm not sure. I swear, I'm not sure. What a miserable excuse for an adult male I am.

Mrs. M.'s voice comes into my ear. *"Choose a girl who is nice. Will you promise me that, Charlie?"*

And I did promise. Although, at the time, I didn't understand why this was suddenly so important to her. *I found somebody who's nice, okay?* I tell her silently. *But I don't know how to do this. I think I might be fucking it up. Could we talk about it? God, I wish we could talk about it.*

SEVEN

In the spring of that awful first year in the bachelor pad, my dad found an article in the Saturday Arts Calendar of our paper about a book signing for a few local authors at a little bookstore in downtown Hudsonville. He waved the article in front of my face and hollered, "This is where it starts, Charlie-boy! This is our foot in the door!"

He called the bookstore, turned on the charm, and within ten minutes had arranged for me to be one of the local authors. They were calling the event Night of the Stars, and I would be there as the youngest star—the youngest published author in history, a kid so enterprising and talented that he had written not one but two books about a beetle, with two more exciting publications on the way. Then Dad called the *Hudsonville Daily* and told them they had mistakenly forgotten to mention me in the article about the local book signing, and he insisted that they should do a separate piece on me and my books by way of apology.

I was sitting on the sofa, listening to these two very different but equally urgent conversations. Up until that moment, the idea that Dad was really going to push me into the spotlight in this crazy-ass way—turn me into a pint-sized celebrity, call me a published author—none of it had seemed real. It was an abstraction. I was not the kind of kid who went for the spotlight in any way. But on that Saturday afternoon, I saw the spotlight coming for me like a big, searching beam, and I also saw that there would be no stopping Dad. He had a dream. It involved books and money and me. My life as a kid nobody noticed was coming to an end. I started chewing my fingernails frantically. Dad startled me by knocking my hand away from my mouth.

"The reporter's coming Monday after school," he said. His voice was tense and determined, as though he expected me to resist. His eyes, as he stared at me, held a trace of panic. I realized that his confidence was flagging now that we were closer to actual liftoff.

"I got this, Dad," I said, although I was way more scared than he was.

"We need to get you a haircut. And maybe a little sport coat. And some business cards. And we have to practice for the interview. We'll have them photograph the first cover and then maybe a photo of you sitting at the computer, writing your next book. Because you were born to write. Can you say that in the interview, Charlie?"

"I was born to write," I repeat.

"Born to it! Unstoppable! Unbelievable! You'll be on the front page, Charlie! Come on, let's get you a haircut. Let's get you dressed for success. Let's rock this town!"

He slicked back his own blond hair and put on a sport coat and changed out of his sneakers. It was, apparently, time for us to dress for success. We left Liam with Valerie, our latest babysitter, and went downtown to buy a suit, get me a haircut, and check in with the nice ladies at the bookstore. In the car, Dad interviewed me and told me the five most important things I needed to say to the bookstore ladies. And the reporter on Monday. And anybody who came up to me at my book signing. They were

- I was born to write (lie).
- I have always loved beetles (lie, scared of bugs).
- I have already sold a lot of books (lie).
- I get straight As in school (big lie).
- I have more books on the way (true).

At one point, Dad got mad at me for stammering. "Are you an idiot? Do I have to explain again how important this interview is? This is *it*, Charlie!"

"Okay," I said. "Okay, okay, okay." I was trying not to cry. I wanted Dad to get his confidence back, but I was so miserable. I had the shortest haircut I had ever had in my life, practically a buzz cut, and I hated the suit Dad had bought for me—it was powder blue—a ridiculous color—and two sizes too big for me so that I could grow into it. It made me realize that in Dad's estimation, this gig was going to last awhile. I would be caught in a jar, on display in that shiny blue suit, for years.

EIGHT

Soon after the wildly successful book signing (we sold forty books), I met Mrs. M. for the first time. It was an author festival on a college campus, somewhere near Grand Rapids—I can't remember exactly where—one of the women who had come to the bookstore had pulled some strings in exchange for a date with Dad. The festival was called Autumn Author Jubilee, and it involved twenty or so authors from all over the state. They were set up with tables all around the edges of the room.

Each table was covered with a white tablecloth and had a stack of books for teachers to purchase on their way around the room. Every author got two metal stands for displaying their newest books. The idea was that all the teachers and librarians would buy tons of books and carry them around in free tote bags supplied by the Jubilee. I had my first two books—*Meet Beetle Boy* and *Beetle Boy Crawls Again*, but my dad had made a poster with the next two book covers on it and "COMING SOON FROM BEETLE BOY" in bright blue letters across the top. We made the poster at the breakfast table with scanned covers that Dad had made on his new scanner, but before we got from the parking lot to the building, everything we had glued onto the poster board had fallen off because we used old glue.

While he unpacked our books, Dad sent me to ask one of the two Jubilee organizers if they had any Scotch tape. One of them found me a roll, and I scurried back to our table. "Hurry it up," Dad ordered. "People are already coming in, and we need to sell fifty books today to pay the rent."

I was taping the book covers back onto the poster board when Mrs. M. arrived; her table was the table beside ours. She was wearing a long black cape and what was pretty obviously a wig—an afro of orange curls. Her face was pasty white. Under her cape, she was wearing a black dress with a trailing skirt. I swear, my first thought was *a witch*. I glanced over at her table, thinking her display book would be a collection of spells and curses. But it was a book called *Franklin Firefly*, with a fat firefly smiling on the cover. My dad saw it the same time I did and looked at me meaningfully. His eyes said, "I'll handle this."

Mrs. M. stepped behind her table, took off her cape, adjusted her wig, and looked around, taking in the meeting room and the other authors at their tables. Finally, she glanced over to the table beside hers—mine. My dad was ready for her, and when her eyes rested on him, he smiled. It was his Caring Man smile. It worked really well on women of all ages.

"Quite a group," he said. "Hope we all sell some books today!"

She looked at my book, took in the fact that it was also a bug book, a fact that seemed to momentarily pain her, but she said, still friendly, "Yes, let's all hope for a good day." She squinted at the book cover and added, "Charlie."

"No, I'm Dan," he said. "Charlie is my boy, here." He sat back in his chair so that she had a clearer sideways view of me. I was wearing the powder-blue suit Dad had bought me for the book signing. I managed a smile. Mrs. M. stared at me for a long moment.

"Charlie's the world's youngest published author," Dad explained.

"Oh, you have got to be kidding me," Mrs. M. said. "Oh, you have really got to be kidding me."

"I'm not kidding!" Dad protested. "My boy here is the world's youngest published author!"

She looked him right in the eye and said, "Your own child. And what is he . . . five?"

"I'm *seven!*" I cried. It hurt me that she thought I was five.

"Be quiet, son," my dad said. "We are not talking to this mean lady."

"No, you certainly are not," she agreed.

Then she marched from her table to the middle of the room where the two organizers were counting the occupied author tables, writing on clipboards. Mrs. M. started talking to them, and she pointed to our table. It was pretty obvious that she was complaining about us. I asked Dad, "Why doesn't she like us?"

"Because she's a bitch. And her book is a piece of crap."

I looked at her book—it had a glossy book jacket and a hard cover. Our books were paperback and very thin. Also, her colors were bright and glossy and ours were dull. The firefly was smiling, and it had teeth like a human's. I thought that was a little strange.

A few minutes later, the two organizer ladies came over and picked up all of Mrs. M.'s books and carried them to another table on the other side of the room, where she had been relocated. The ladies seemed embarrassed. My dad put on his best Caring Man smile and asked the prettier one, "Does she have something against little children?"

"She's a character, that Martha," the pretty one said. She was wearing a tight pink turtleneck.

The other lady said, "Always fussing about something."

"Maybe you shouldn't invite her next time," my dad suggested helpfully.

Pink Turtleneck said, "Maybe not."

My dad was smiling as they walked away, a triumphant smile, like the smile he always wore after he'd won an argument with Mom, using male logic. "She won't be invited again," he said. "But we will."

"Way to go, Dad."

But I couldn't help watching Mrs. M. during the rest of the Author Jubilee, sitting behind her new table on the other side of the room. She looked small, although when she had been glaring at us, I had the impression she was huge! *Maybe she is a witch*, I thought. I was already in awe of her. She had insulted my dad. He muttered something about her under his breath every few minutes.

Another author had set up camp on the other side of my table—a young guy named Dr. Naturo, who didn't have a book at all. He had a DVD of songs, and he had brought a guitar with him. His DVD was called *Nature—It's a Natural!* His poster said that he had visited schools all over the state and that he had a website full of fun activities for kids. My dad moved his chair over behind Dr. Naturo's table and talked to him for a whole hour, leaving me alone. I knew that Dad was getting ideas from him—he called it networking—and I was nervous. I wanted so badly to bite my fingernails, but Dad told me before we left the apartment that if I bit my fingernails in public he would make me wear gloves like a girl.

Dr. Naturo didn't get any school invitations that day, although a few people took his card. We only sold six books in two hours. Mrs. M. wasn't selling books either; I watched her. I overheard Pink Turtleneck telling another organizer that none of the teachers or librarians had as much money this year and that only about half as many teachers came to the conference. My dad had stepped away from our table to get a plate of food for us from the lunch buffet. When he came back, he sat down beside me with a plate and two forks and said to several organizers within earshot, "What a nice conference this is. Good job, everybody." He was forcing a smile, hiding his disappointment at our sales.

I wanted to tell him what I had just overheard, but now he was busy making serious eye contact with Pink Turtleneck. She came closer. "Your son is adorable," she said. "I read about him in the paper—what an enterprising little guy—writing books already!"

My dad widened his eyes at me, and so I said quickly, "I was born to write."

"He's just getting started . . . ," Dad prompted.

"Two more on the way!" My voice cracked when I said this though, because I was tired. But Pink Turtleneck didn't notice; she was still batting her eyes at my dad.

He didn't say anything else about Mrs. M. until we got into

our car. Then he said with a snarl, "I cannot *believe* the nerve of that bitch in the cape. She stole our mojo, son! She muddied the water! But she'll be sorry she messed with me. Oh, she'll be sorry!"

"Well, actually," I began explaining, "I heard that the reason that the teachers weren't buying was—"

"Next time we see her we'll squash her but good!"

"Like a bug," I said, trying to make him laugh.

"Hell *yes*, like a bug." he roared. He stuck his thumb high in the air and brought it down onto the dashboard, squashing Mrs. M. but good for ruining our day.

NINE

So weren't you and your little brother ever close, Charlie?

"Um . . . no."

Weren't you at least close when you were little guys?

"Not really."

It's just really hard for me to figure this out because . . . well . . . my whole life I wanted a little brother. I used to beg my parents for a little brother. I still want one! It's so hard for me to imagine having one that you don't even stay in touch with.

Of course she was confused. It wasn't normal to be out of touch with my only brother. But I couldn't begin to explain all the ways that I had hurt Liam. He lives with Mom now, irony of ironies—Mom moved back to Grand Rapids after I moved out of Green Grove. She got custody of Liam and put him in a private school. And here's another irony—turns out Liam is a musical genius. He's fifteen, a sophomore, and he's going to transfer to a school for musical geniuses any minute now. How do I know this? I read it in the paper. Liam started playing the violin a few years before I ditched him. Some teacher took pity on him and hooked him up with an instrument and a private teacher in Grand Rapids.

Clara is waiting for me to respond. I move my hand to the springy ponytail at the back of her head, burying my fingers in the hair around the ring of elastic. I put my face close to the nape of her neck and sniff deeply. Her hair is fragrant, musky, and female. I don't want to talk anymore about Liam. But she pulls away, out of reach, and I am stuck in my cast and can't recover her.

Charlie, he's your brother.

"We went through a really bad time," I say. "And then we just couldn't be normal brothers anymore."

Because of your mom abandoning you?

I had never used that word: *abandon*. It surprises me to hear it spoken by Clara, but I nod. Although I had been thinking that the reason we couldn't be normal was more about me—because I mocked him. Worse, because I didn't protect him. Worse, because I left him. If I was Liam, I would never forgive me.

But he has obviously forgiven Mom after she came back to Michigan and took Liam away from Dad and Ruby. Have I mentioned Ruby?

Clara said once, "I know I'm not your first girlfriend. I know you've been in other relationships."

"Not like this," I said, and I meant not in a sane way. More in a depraved, pathetic, crippled way. A string of babysitters, ending with Ruby Mandarino. A pastiche of pretty girls to pester and woo with my premature charm and my lonely heart. But Ruby was hired primarily to deal with Liam, since I was beyond needing a babysitter. I never really got her attention. She liked Dad a little too much. She was the beginning of the end of the three amigos.

◆ ◆ ◆

Young Dr. Naturo was a fountain of information for Dad; I guess they totally hit if off once he learned that Dad had a run-in with Mrs. M. at the Author's Jubilee. According to the Doctor, Mrs. M. had a reputation for being negative and unreasonable at the local author conferences. I guess one time Mrs. M. asked the Doctor why he even considered himself an author when all he ever wrote were bad songs that nobody ever heard except kids in school who were trapped into it. He told Dad that she was jealous because he was making so much money on his school visits, during which he could sometimes sell over a hundred homemade CDs at ten dollars a pop.

All of this Dad relayed to me with great excitement—he saw instantly that our future was in school visits. But I was more curious about Mrs. M. "Then why is she even invited to those author deals?"

The Doctor told Dad that she won some big book award, so now everybody feels obligated to include her, and she keeps showing up, pissing off the organizers with her demands. According to the Doctor, she was a total has-been.

I had never heard that term before, and I asked Dad what it meant. "Someone who used to be important. So everybody is just playing along at the conferences, but nobody really gives a shit about her stupid books anymore."

When I heard this, I thought to myself, *Maybe someday no one will give a shit about my stupid books either.* The thought filled me with a shiny, piercing hope.

◆ ◆ ◆

The next time I saw Mrs. M. was at another Saturday morning author celebration, this one in a high school gymnasium. I was half a dozen tables away from her and her *Franklin Firefly* books; I couldn't stop myself from wandering over to her while my dad was out of sight.

"Not you again," she said. "Shouldn't you be home watching cartoons?"

"I'm here because I'm the—

"World's youngest published author, I remember. But aren't you supposed to stay away from me?"

"My dad went for coffee with one of the organizers," I explained. "He said he won't be back for fifteen minutes."

"Probably looking for a closet."

"What?"

"I'd hurry back to your table if I were you."

I wasn't eager to go back. "Can I ask you something? Why does your firefly have teeth? Don't you know that fireflies don't have teeth?"

She looked down at me, one of her eyebrows arched way up. "Where is your mother, World's Youngest Published Author? And why haven't I ever seen her at any of these meat markets?"

The question caught me off guard. I confessed abruptly, "She's gone."

"Dead?"

"No. Just . . . gone. We can't . . . we don't talk about her."

"Who is 'we'?"

"Me, my dad, and my little brother, Liam."

"And how long exactly has your mother been gone? A few months? A year?"

"Let me get back to you on that," I said.

Back at my table, I watched Dad come back into the gym with a couple of teachers. One of them was wearing a white lacy top that you could see her black bra through.

"Here's my boy!" Dad exclaimed, presenting me and the books. "Say hello, Charlie. These wonderful ladies wanted to meet the world's youngest published author."

"Hello," I said.

"Did you get any new ideas while I was gone?" Dad prompted.

"Oh, I find inspiration everywhere," I said, another totally phony thing I had been coached to say.

"Well, isn't he something!" Visible Black Bra said. She picked up a copy of *Meet Beetle Boy*, opened it, scanned a few pages, and exclaimed, "This is too cute!"

The other woman was middle-aged and seemed more skeptical. She was reading *Beetle Boy Crawls Again*. "Your son is how old?"

"Seven, going on fifteen—ha-ha."

"Does he have an agent?"

I wasn't sure what an agent was. I looked at Dad; he was stuck in a private smile with VBB. She said admiringly,

"Seems like you two are doing okay without one!"

They bought five books between them. Then I had a lull. Dad went off to look for more pretty teachers, and I took out a small pad of scratch paper and counted up the number of months I had lived since Mom left. I included the month before she actually moved out because I hardly saw her that month. Fourteen months. It was the first time I had allowed myself to tally up this terrible number. Then I just had to tell someone. I waited until Dad left the conference hall to hit the deli across the street from the conference hotel, and then I left my table and scurried back over to Mrs. M.'s table. "Fourteen months," I said.

She didn't miss a beat. "Well, well. Right around the time these books started materializing." She looked away from me and said to no one in particular, "What a miserable profession this has become. Broken, broken people."

"Excuse me," I objected. "I am not broken. I've sold eighteen books today, and my dad said I only had to sell fifteen."

"Well, at least your pimp is having a good day."

"What?"

"Go back to your table. You're not supposed to talk to me."

"They're her stories," I blurted. "They're the stories my mom used to tell us at bedtime. To help us get to sleep."

Mrs. M. sighed. "The pimping deepens."

"What?"

"Oh, we're all pimps, Charlie. Pretending to care about our sad little readers. Pretending our silly stories help them."

"I don't think they help," I said, another huge confession. "They sure aren't helping me."

She looked down at me again, and her eyes were not as hard

and beady as usual. She looked almost kind. I wanted to ask her if we could talk again sometime. I wasn't even sure she liked me, but she was the only person in my life who knew a little bit of what was happening to me.

But I was also afraid of what would happen if Dad saw me talking to her. So I said, "Well, okay, gotta go. Good luck with your writing."

Mrs. M. called as I hurried away, "Good luck with your childhood."

TEN

It's Saturday morning. We both slept in, and I'd had no night-mares. I feel more refreshed than usual, and Clara decides to make ginger pancakes, which I'd never even heard of until I met her and which now seem like another of her many generosities. She stands at the stove in a short blue bathrobe with her feet bare and her toes turning slightly in. I watch her and think about maybe trying to have sex with her after breakfast, lying across her bed on my good side with very little movement and the entire beautiful back of Clara inspiring me onward. It might work. Right after breakfast.

But Clara ruins my mood with her next statement, spoken while handing me a plate of perfect pancakes.

Charlie, I can tell that you're a very private person, and I want to respect your privacy, but lately I can't help feeling like I'm being shut out. I want . . . I need you to start telling me more about your life. Your family. What happened back then? I get that it was hard. But I need to know more. Maybe I can help you. Maybe things could get better. Now that you have . . . me.

Now that I have Clara. What does that even mean? Do I have Clara? If I do, am I under obligation to hand over everything—all the ugliness and confusion, all the secrets, all the lies? All the reasons I am so alone?

Where are your friends? I hear Clara wondering. *Give me a reason to believe you're a normal person.*

"Great pancakes," I say. "Best batch ever."

This makes her angry. She stands up and brings her face close to mine.

Did you hear even one word I said, Charlie Porter?

I am silent, scrambling for a way out of this conversation. A sudden leg spasm? A migraine? An attack of indigestion? To my surprise, Clara grabs my plate, sweeps it up, and steps away from me. She is withdrawing her pancakes. And she is on the verge of tears. I haven't seen her cry since she came to the hospital after my accident, and it unhinges me.

"Oh, God, OKAY! I heard you. I heard you. I know I've been kind of . . . a closed book. It's just . . . it's just . . . I've never been in a relationship like this before. Where the other person wants to know *everything*."

I say the last word a little accusingly, and she surprised me again by exploding angrily.

Don't say it like that. I am not asking you to tell me everything. I'm asking you to tell me the basics. Believe me, Charlie, stuff about your parents and your only living

brother—those are the basics. *You could have a different ex-girlfriend on every street of this town, and I don't care about that. I don't care if you have a criminal record. I don't care if you traveled all over Europe and you forgot to mention it. I just want the BASICS!*

I have never seen her angry like this. I want it to stop. "Okay, okay, you don't have to yell. I'll try harder. I promise I'll try harder. Can I have my pancakes back?"

I hear myself and think, *Am I nine? Is she going to send me to my room now?*

She still has the plate in one hand, aloft. She is not backing down. She is wearing an unfamiliar, matronly frown. She wants one important revelation before pancakes.

I put my hands over my eyes and release a little groan of submission and then say, "When I was little, I did some really mean things to my brother. And he had nobody but me to help him. So now I can't face him. It hurts me to even say his name. Maybe that's why I have dreams about him sometimes. Okay?"

Clara's expression changes, becomes a combination of gratitude and dismay. She puts the plate back in front of me, and now her voice is quiet.

You can't always have been mean to him. That's not the Charlie I know. You must have been a good brother sometimes.

"I was a terrible brother," I insist. I want her to believe it. I had never admitted it to anyone before, not even Mrs. M.

◆ ◆ ◆

I don't know who Dad had to sleep with to get me the author

gig at the state capitol, but somehow, in my second year of being the youngest published author in the history of mankind, I got invited to Lansing with four other authors to meet the governor. I kid you not—the governor of Michigan. I was eight years old, but I looked younger; I was unnaturally small, the smallest kid in my class, because I had started school so early. Clara has told me several times how little I was when I came to her school, like a bug. She says it makes her want to cry, remembering me. It makes me want to throw a chair against a wall.

But back to my trip to Lansing. My dad was crazed with excitement for two weeks; he kept calling it my big break and saying it would put us over the top—wrong on both counts—but he did warn me, dropping his enthusiasm for a moment, that unfortunately the old has-been was going to be one of the four other authors.

"Why did they even invite her if she's such a has-been?" I wondered, hiding that I was glad she would be there.

"Who knows? She wrote some hotshot book that won some hotshot award one hundred years ago, and she's still milking it. None of the women I've met at author stuff can stand her."

I made a mental note to find out what the hotshot book was when I have my next moment alone with her, hopefully during my visit to the capitol as the youngest living published American author.

◆ ◆ ◆

The Lansing gig was super easy—only a half day, no performance, no anxiety attacks, and no hassles. We didn't get paid anything, but Dad said it was fantastic free publicity. Mrs. M. and I were two of five authors invited; we were at opposite ends of the age spectrum, and the three other authors—one man and two ladies—were more like Dad's age, and one of them was pretty, so Dad went right to work on her, but he didn't wander too far because his big goal for the day was to get a photo of me with the governor of Michigan to put on my future website.

In those days, the governor of Michigan was really beautiful. She is now history, but back then, I remember that she made a big fuss over me and asked me where I get my ideas. I was too unglued to answer her, which Dad lambasted me about later. But we all got to be in a group shot photograph with her and a bunch of other state politicians and staffers. Then she gave a little speech about literacy and children being our top natural resources ("blah, blah, blah," Mrs. M. said, loud enough for people besides me to hear, I swear). But then came the moment that Dad had been praying for, if you can call his manipulating and conning praying. The governor actually agreed to let him take one picture of just her and me—the leader of our state and the world's youngest and most miserable and neurotic published author.

I got the distinct impression that day that the other authors were seriously annoyed by both me and my dad. I overheard one of the two women authors saying, "Did you notice the dad moves his lips when the kid is talking? Like a puppeteer!"

I met Mrs. M.'s eyes; she had heard this too. "It's true, Charlie."

"The governor liked him," I reminded her.

"She knows a good photo op when she sees one," Mrs. M. said. "It's called politics."

"I was wondering about something, Mrs. M.," I said. "I was wondering what your book was that won that big award."

Her expression changed. She looked suspicious. "Why were you wondering that?" she asked.

"I was thinking I might buy one," I said.

Sarcastic again. "Oh, that would help me out so much."

I asked, frustrated, "Why do you even *come* to these deals? My dad *makes* me come. Nobody makes *you* come."

"You have a good point there, Charlie."

"It seems like you don't even like being an author. Do you have to do this because you're poor?"

This made her pause. She stroked her chin, thinking. "My husband's premature death was a bit of a financial complication," she admitted. "But I am not poor."

"He died? How did he die?"

"Poor lovely man. He fell out of a boat. Hit his head, knocked himself out, and drowned."

"Was it a long time ago?"

"Ten years."

"Didn't you have any kids?"

"No kids."

"Didn't you want kids?"

This question actually made her smile. Was it the first smile I had seen on her pale, puffy-eyed face? Had I actually amused her? She said, "I hate kids, remember?"

"I never said that!"

"Oops. I confused you with a certain relative. No, I never had kids, and no, I don't regret it."

I had no trouble believing this, even at eight. "But you do miss your husband sometimes."

"All the time. Every single day. But I'm doing okay without him."

"I'm doing okay without my mom," I whispered.

"You are *not*, Charlie," she scolded. "You need your mom. And she shouldn't have left you. Don't be so blind."

I was astounded. I couldn't believe she would say something so mean. But she didn't look mean. She just looked sure. All the same, I was suddenly very angry. And what I said next was something straight out of Dan Porter's Book of Life. "You're the one who's blind!" I cried. "You don't have any sense at all! And you're prejudiced against boys!"

She snorted with amusement. "Go away, if I'm so prejudiced against boys."

"I am never going to speak to you, ever AGAIN!"

"My heart is broken. Go write another book, why don't you? It should take you ten minutes."

We stared at each other. I think we were both surprised by our own nastiness. I broke the silence and asked, more normally, "How long does it take you to write your books?"

"I don't know," she said. "I'm basically in a coma when I write them."

"What's a coma?"

"You'll know when you're in one. Go back over to your dad now. He's getting way too friendly with the folktale lady from Traverse City." I looked over at him. It was true. He hadn't even noticed that I was talking to the forbidden Mrs. M.

"I didn't mean it when I said I wouldn't talk to you anymore."

"My prayers are answered. See you at the next author strip show."

"What?"

"Just GO."

I skittered away.

ELEVEN

I am back in the Green Grove Apartment, searching for a hidden stash of book money, something I can give Clara for letting me live with her. Underwear and clothes are strewn in every room, worst in the bedroom where I find my filthy unmade bed. Hanging by a nail above the bed is the plaque from the governor of Michigan, naming me as a top Michigan author. I realize that if I show the plaque to my mom she might forgive me for stealing her stories. It's not too late. I kneel on the bed and pull the plaque off the wall and see that behind it is a hole packed with bills—the book money! I reach up to start pulling the bills out but then quickly draw it back, aware of a sudden whirring noise, aware of the danger of poking my arm into a hole in that place, the apartment, that bedroom. It's a trap!

I sit up and say out loud, "It's a trap!"

Oops. It's the middle of the night, and Clara is watching me, standing in the doorway to her bedroom.

What's a trap, Charlie?

I don't answer. I fall backward onto the mattress and fake

snore, pretending to be instantly back asleep.

◆ ◆ ◆

It's evening, and now Clara is standing just inside the front door, twisting her hands and stammering. She has been gone from the apartment for two hours on a weeknight, something that has not happened, ever. I am both relieved that she is back and also anxious because she is clearly searching for words to tell me something she thinks I won't want to hear.

Charlie, listen to me. Listen to me a minute. There's something . . . there's something I really need to tell you, and I don't want you to get mad at me. Are you listening? Do you promise not to get mad?

For the first time since I moved in with her a month ago, she looks afraid. Of me. I ease my cast down off the ottoman so that I can sit more normally. She is wearing a floral T-shirt and a skirt to her ankles, relatively dressed up. Her cheeks are flushed.

"I thought you were just getting groceries," I say. "What took you so long?"

She twists her hands, grimacing. What am I feeling? An old dread. Something new, coming to crush me.

Okay, I didn't actually go to the store. I went . . . I went . . . to a concert instead, Charlie. A violin concert in Grand Rapids by all these young local musicians. And there was one boy playing the violin, and he had a solo. And his name was Liam.

"So what?" I snap, suddenly angry. "I told you my brother was a musician."

Oh my God, Charlie, he played the most beautiful sonata. It was Bach. It was to die for.

"Where are you going with this, Clara? Are you upset that I don't play a musical instrument?"

Charlie, I stayed in the auditorium after the concert because I wanted to see him up close. And then I milled around backstage and people were leaving and there I was basically spying on this boy, this boy who doesn't look anything like you, but then I saw this older woman come up to him and she gave him a hug, and Charlie, when she turned around, I knew it was your mother. Her hair, her eyes, her mouth. I knew it was her.

"So *what*, Clara? You saw my mother, so what?"

I don't know . . . it was just . . . haven't you ever wanted to just call her?

She already knows the answer to this question. She is shaking her head, disagreeing with my answer. I know what is coming. I know the sort of thing Clara would have done at the first sighting of my brother and my mother. Helpful, kindhearted Clara. I picture her moving in her skippy, bright-eyed way over to them. They would hold back at first—reserved and uncertain—*Charlie's girlfriend?* But she would convince them and win them over—it would happen quickly, especially Liam. I close my eyes, unhappy beyond words at this picture in my mind.

Anyway . . . I told them I'm your girlfriend. I told them that you're staying in my apartment while your leg heals.

I picture Mom. I hear her voice. "How did Charles break

his leg?" She was the only person who ever called me Charles. Clara would explain, "He was running out of a house, and he stumbled and tore his Achilles tendon and just fell down in the street." She would touch her own ankle, her expression grave.

Your mom seemed upset to hear about your leg, Charlie. She couldn't even speak for a minute. I thought she was going to cry. I felt so bad for her.

"Spare me."

Your brother didn't say anything. He was just watching your mom. Like he was concerned for her. Then she sort of pulled herself together, and she asked me how long we've known each other.

Clara would have updated her happily. "We met at Rite Aid, where I work. We liked each other right away. Then Charlie tore his Achilles tendon, and he's in a cast so he needed to move in with me. Now, we live together, and we know each other in the biblical sense."

No, Clara would not have said this part, although she could have; Mom would have no business objecting, despite her religious beliefs. She has no parental authority over me. She has no right to act like my mother.

Clara is getting more nervous, sensing my disapproval of what she is telling me. Sensing my unwillingness to picture a scene that includes this impossible threesome. Her voice fades to a whisper, and she is starting to grimace, tic-like. All very out of character. The Porters have infected her with their powerful germs.

"Would you just stop cringing and get to the point?"

This centers her. She calms down. She steps to the plate. She swings.

The point is that I invited them to come over to see you.

"Oh, no, you didn't," I say. "That is not possible. Not a chance. Not gonna happen."

They said yes, *Charlie! They both said yes right away, like there was no question in their minds—*

I close my eyes. I cover my ears. Not here. Not like this. Not with my leg in a cast. Not both of them together.

Charlie!

Clara sits beside me on the sofa and does something that kills me. She takes my hands away from my ears and lowers them to my lap and then puts one of her small hands right over my heart.

I will help you with this. We'll move things forward a little bit, that's all. You and me. That's all I'm asking.

"Clara, NO!"

Let them come here with me by your side. Then never again, if that's what you decide. Just this one time. To move us forward.

And I realize something about Clara. She isn't only cheery sweetness. She gets an idea, and she stays with it. She has a position. She believes in family. She has always wanted a brother. She has forgiven my unforgivable mother. It's a grave complication. I don't know where to go with it.

"No," I say, but it was like it wasn't even me saying it anymore. It was too late. It was done.

◆ ◆ ◆

Later, I have the most vivid memory of being in Mrs. M.'s house, almost like a vision. Why? Because Liam and Mom are moving toward me? While Mrs. M. is gone? I was there, in her kitchen, making the morning coffee. Mrs. M. had taught me how to make it—beans ground in a grinder, filtered water, a good brand of coffee, but not too dark roasted. I grew to like it her way—my dad drank only generic already-ground coffee from a tin, bitter and weak at the same time. He drank the terrible stuff all day. But Mrs. M.'s morning coffee was wonderful.

Her kitchen had Asian-inspired wallpaper—cartoon cranes and rabbits and lotus blossoms—and she had a little green vinyl booth in one corner, like a personal restaurant. This was where I would sit and sip coffee and get ready to face the school day. There was a high window above the booth that showed a maple tree. Birds flew back and forth from the tree's lower branches to the window feeders, and Mrs. M. knew the names of all the birds—I swear, anything that flew by—she could tell me what it was. She wasn't crabby in the mornings, and she seemed to like that I had learned to make her coffee exactly right. She always wore an old bathrobe that was a faded purple plaid and her hair would be matted in the back because she slept on her back and her face would be softer and her voice huskier.

Are you ready for school, Charlie? Did you have a good day? Do you need anything before I go to bed?

I am falling into sleep. *No beetle dreams*, I instruct my unconscious. But of course there is a dream.

I am in Clara's kitchen, my own age, but in this dream I haven't written the books yet and I know I have to write them because I need money. I am under tremendous pressure to get all eight of them written in a few days or else I will have to move back in with Dad and Liam. I am trying to begin when I realize that it is impossible for me to write the books without Mom. Then I am on a train, and I am going to Wisconsin to get beetle stories directly from Mom. The train turns into a rowboat. I have nothing with me but an old trash bag full of clothes and one book—*Franklin Firefly,* the one where Franklin has a cold and he can't stop sneezing out his lights. I open the book to the first page, and there is a message for me in Mrs. M.'s handwriting, instructions for what to say to my mother. The message says, *Tell your mother you will bring the biggest beetle to her house and she will have to take care of it.* I close the book, very nervous in the boat now, unable to row, unsure that I will be able to deliver this message to my mother, unsure of how I could ever get the gigantic beetle to Wisconsin, upset with Mrs. M. for giving me an impossible task instead of helping me.

TWELVE

I can't safely stand on a footstool with my cast, so instead, I tap the edge of the box above me with the end of my crutch, patiently, firmly, until it moves far enough forward to fall into my arms. My project: relocate boxes before Clara comes home. I open the box in my arms, flipping through its contents, straightening the items that were mixed up in the fall. Then I close the lid, tuck the box under one arm, and reorient myself with my crutch.

As I am backing out of Clara's closet, I brush against a long dressy skirt made of black velvet—a fabric I hate. In fact, the sensation of velvet against my arm sends me reeling into another memory—I am nine years old and inside my new costume, and there is no escape, no way to get myself out of reach from my dad's latest idea for selling books—a beetle costume hand-sewn by someone named Dorothy, who also made several sets of ugly curtains for us before Dad got tired of her.

The costume probably earned Dorothy an extra two weeks

of attention from Dad—it was carefully designed and sewn with six black legs, a thickly padded body, and black velvet wings. On my feet were black sneakers. Dorothy had also created a black helmet that tied under my chin and had thick pipe cleaners at the top of my head for antennae. Dad was thrilled—he made me put it on immediately and watched me skulking around in it, all the while grabbing and snuggling with Dorothy, who was beaming with pride, not noticing or not caring that I was itching my neck and generally acting miserable.

"You're a real bug now, Charlie!" Dad crowed. "We are going to kick so much ass at the next author program. Excuse my French, Dorothy."

"It's irritating my neck," I pleaded.

"It's perfect, son. Stop sniveling and thank Dorothy for all her hard work on your costume."

"When is his next official author presentation?" Dorothy asked hopefully. She had never seen one and expected now to be invited as the costume designer. She didn't know that she would be out of the picture before the end of the month.

◆ ◆ ◆

Dad had scheduled me for a big author festival at an elementary school in Kalamazoo, right after the school year started. This got me off to a very bad start with my third-grade teacher, who—big surprise—did not approve of me missing school, even if I was the world's youngest published author. The necessity of defying her, along with the size of the audience (my first auditorium), and the added discomfort and humiliation of the costume, made me a quaking, sweating, skin-erupting mess in the minutes before my presentation. Through a haze of fear, I saw the familiar A-lined shape of Mrs. M., dressed in black, talking to a librarian. I flitted over to her and tugged at her skirt.

"Mother of God," she said, looking down at me. "He's making your wear a *costume* now?" She looked around for him, ready to fight.

"Don't say anything about it," I begged. "He's in a really bad mood."

Then I started to really cry. I took hold of her skirt with both hands and put my face into the fabric and just broke down. Mrs. M. saw that I was at the end of my rope. She leaned down and lifted my face gently away from her skirt, which now had a big shiny circle on it from my tears. She cupped my wet chin in her hand and put her own face right up close to mine, shutting out the rest of the world, the kids in the hall, the smiling teachers, the fawning librarian, the angrily approaching father. Her hand on my chin was warm. Her breath in my face was warm. She spoke very calmly, just to me: "I will make this work for you today. Stay close to me. If you feel confused about what to do, just look at me. I'll make it work. I am in charge of you today."

I am in charge of you today.

"Okay," I blubbered.

"Wipe your tears now," she said, handing me a Kleenex from the pocket of her black cardigan. "No one has seen them but me."

A shadow fell over us. "Get away from my boy," Dad growled.

Mrs. M. gave the side of my face one last meaningful pat, and then she straightened up and addressed my father. "Are you talking to me, Mr. Porter? Are you TALKING to me? I thought we had an agreement about that, sir."

"I said stay away from my BOY."

"I am PERFORMING with him, Mr. Porter. We are scheduled to perform TOGETHER. So I can't very well stay away from him, can I?"

She took my hand and said to the librarian: "Lead on, dear! We are ready to inspire your young readers!"

We were led away, down the hall, heading to the auditorium. Behind us, I could hear my dad exclaiming and asking angry questions about why I was performing with another author instead of alone. Mrs. M. held fast to my sweaty hand. The tears had dried on my cheeks. I let myself be led. If she had picked me up and carried me in her arms onto the stage, I wouldn't have objected. I felt—what can I say?—*rescued*. I was with Mama Bug.

We walked into the spotlight together. There was a mic on a stand and a wireless mic. Mrs. M. attached the wireless mic to my costume and looked deeply into my eyes, asking me wordlessly if I was ready to begin. The auditorium had gone completely silent. I nodded.

"My name is Martha Manning," she said grandly, and she threw open her arms, embracing all the kids in the auditorium—about two hundred first-, second-, and third-graders. They broke into spontaneous applause. "And THIS," she paused dramatically. "This is my special friend, Beetle Boy. Is he not magnificent, with his black wings and his quivering antennae?"

I was leaning into Mrs. M.'s skirt like a four-year-old. I gave the audience a little wave. Again, applause.

"Beetle Boy is here to tell you a story! A story from his life under the ground, before he came here today to your wonderful school."

She turned to me again, clasping her hands in delight at the story I was about to tell. The story I had spent half the night memorizing. Of course, I had forgotten every word. I looked at Mrs. M. in alarm, communicating this, and somehow, somehow, she understood and produced a copy of *Meet Beetle Boy*, pulling it from the floppy pocket of her cardigan. She opened it as though it were a sacred scroll and held it up in the air. "Do you want to hear how our story begins?" she asked the students.

They did! They were already cheering to hear the beginning of my stupid story.

Mrs. M. handed me the book with a flourish, opened to the first page. "Tell us your story, Beetle Boy!" she commanded.

I took it from her and focused on the words, and I opened my mouth and out came the opening sentence: "One day, the dirt all around me was especially yucky, and I needed to be in some nice clean grass for a change. So I began to crawl."

Beside me, Mrs. M. began to swim through the air with her back hunched over. The kids went wild—like it was the funniest thing they had ever seen.

"I crawled and I crawled and I crawled. Pretty soon, I saw the sun peeking through a hole in the dirt. Then I was in the sun and it was cool."

You get the picture. Stupid book, cute kid in a costume, crazy lady acting like a crawling bug. A total hit! The auditorium kept bursting into applause. When I finished reading my story, it was pandemonium. Then I answered questions from the audience, Mrs. M. smiling at me and leading the kids into easy, safe territory. She was in charge.

Then we were finished! The school librarian gave me a big squishy hug, and even my dad didn't seem angry anymore, although he wouldn't make eye contact with Mrs. M., which I'm sure was fine with her. My dad got handed a big check from the librarian for seventy-five preordered books. After that, he was in a rush to leave, and he started pulling me by the arm from the gymnasium to the school entrance.

I was looking around for Mrs. M., realizing she hadn't even mentioned her own book during the presentation. I wondered if she needed to sell books to pay rent like we did. I wanted to ask her if she needed some of the money. But Dad was pulling me by the arm away from the school and into the parking lot, toward our car. Then I saw Mrs. M. off to one side of the parking lot, sitting inside her little blue hatchback with her head lowered over the steering wheel. She did not look up. I wanted so much to thank her, but Dad was basically dragging me to the opposite side of the lot. He was beside himself with excitement about selling seventy-five books at one school.

He was probably thinking, How many schools could we actually hit in a single day . . . Four? Five?

I was thinking, *I didn't die. I didn't die.*

◆ ◆ ◆

In the days following my auditorium triumph, the need to thank Mrs. M. grew inside of my heart like a weed. On a Saturday, I snuck some money out of the grocery fund and walked by myself a mile and a half to the downtown office supply store and bought her a present—a pen in a case with a row of diamonds on the clip. It felt like the perfect gift, one author to another. Thank you for preventing the total annihilation of my identity, Mrs. M.

After the auditorium gig, my dad bitched for weeks about

how that has-been had stolen the spotlight from me because she was so jealous and such an old hag and a few worse things. I, on the other hand, was hiding my present of ink and diamonds in the pocket of my coat, taking it everywhere I went. Each time I looked at it, I could relive that sweet moment when Mrs. M. had said, with her hot breath and her steely voice, "*I am in charge of you today.*"

◆ ◆ ◆

Clara set up the reunion quickly—for the next Thursday, her day off, at 3 p.m., right after Liam "gets out of school." Like she is suddenly so aware of his schedule.

Will your mom be free around that time?

I do not know or care what Mom does with her days, but this is one of several things Clara is asking me and my answer is always the same.

"No idea."

What kind of cookies does she like?

"No idea."

Does she drink coffee or tea?

"No idea."

Is she cool about us living together?

This question puts me over the top. "Jesus, Clara! Do you think for one minute that I care what my mother thinks about us living together?"

Don't yell at me, Charlie! I'm doing this for you!

I completely snap. "Oh my God! You are not doing this for me! You are so not doing this for me! This whole thing makes me want to jump out of a window and break my other leg! Maybe then I could be in a hospital, and I wouldn't have to watch you getting all mixed up with stuff that's none of your BUSINESS!"

She put her hands up to her face as though I had slapped her, her face mushing into tears. God, I hate, hate, hate it when people cry. If I hadn't been in a cast and unable to move quickly, I would have lurched for the door and run away.

Instead, I mumble, "Sorry, sorry, overreacting, can't help it." I hold out my arms to her guiltily. She shakes her head through her tears, refusing my hug.

If you're my boyfriend, then this is my business, Charlie. That's how it works if you want to be in a relationship with me.

"I'm already in a relationship with you! I'm doing the best I can! I'm trying to tell you I'm not ready for this, Clara. You won't listen to me."

I listened to you. I am totally here for you. But I just think—

"You think everything is so simple. God, you think people can just . . . forget the past if they all sit down and eat cookies together! Well, it's not like that with the Porter family! Nothing good will come of this visit. It is not a good idea!"

She has listened to this, but now she wipes her eyes, calm again, back in charge.

Well, Charlie, I invited them, and I can't just uninvite them. We have to go through with it. If it doesn't go well, we won't have to ever do it again. And for your information, I do not think everything is simple. I know there's a lot of sad stuff in your past that you don't want to talk about. I'm trying to be patient. But the opportunity arose for a visit, and I decided to be open to it and make an effort, just like you made an effort with my family. Now, would you just please tell me . . . does your mom drink tea or coffee?

"Clara, I swear to God, I honestly don't know. I don't know if my mom drinks coffee or tea. And I don't care."

But then later, maybe because of the questions, I start to remember little things. I remembered a teapot. It was china blue and had some significance—someone in her past had given it to her—her own mother? My mom drank tea. A special tea for her asthma. Another tea for her nervous stomach. And then I remembered that she was a vegetarian and that my dad hated her cooking and sometimes went out for fast food by himself after she had cooked something healthy for him. And I remembered that she made her own soap and put almond oil in our bathwater. And that she played hymns on the guitar, but only when we were in bed, so that I would sometimes hear her singing as I was falling asleep. I did not want to remember these things. They were pointless details of a lost time. They added to my dread. I was pinned.

***

Mrs. M. came to her front door in an unrecognizable form. She was wearing a baggy blue cardigan over a white blouse and ordinary jeans. No wig! Her hair was very short, as short as mine, and gray-blond. She did not look like a witch. She looked completely normal, like somebody's plain old grandmother. She also did not look particularly happy to see me.

"What in the world? Charlie? How in God's name did you get here?"

"Dial-a-Ride," I said. "Easy, breezy."

"Who told you where I live?"

"You're in the phone book, Mrs. M.! I can use a phone book, I'm nine years old. May I come in?"

"You may . . . you may . . . come in," she said warily. "But why do you *want* to come in?"

"I brought you something," I said. I patted my pocket, where the diamond pen rested. I pressed myself through the door and walked past her, into her house.

"Is your brother home alone?" she asked. A pattern was forming; she often asked me about Liam, and I didn't like it.

"He's fine. He's with the new babysitter."

Her house was surprisingly normal—a one-story ranch with a small, shady front porch and a fenced-in backyard. As she led me from the front door to the kitchen, I craned my neck like an owl, taking it all in—the wooden floors, the colorful throw rugs, dark red pleated shades on the windows. It was really nice. Comfortable. Not trashed, like our apartment, but also not too clean. Kind of busy. Cozy. Mrs. M. had projects—knitting baskets, sewing baskets, stacks of books, a jigsaw puzzle on a table, halfway done—hummingbirds in a garden. I noticed that her furniture looked old, but not dirty. Her kitchen had beautiful wallpaper and a skylight and the kitchen windows had white curtains. White curtains! I was acting nonchalant, but the details of her house filled me with happiness. Mrs. M. invited me to sit at her corner breakfast nook—green vinyl seats and a paisley tablecloth. I plunked down and smoothed the fabric in front of me with both hands. Amazing. Clean. I was very hungry, but I sensed I might be pushing it to ask for food.

Mrs. M. was watching me. "Is everything all right today, Charlie?"

"Oh sure. Everything all right with you?"

"Why are you here?"

"I told you, I *brought* you something. And you weren't at the last author conference. That big one in Grand Rapids. I looked for you."

"Did something bad happen to you at that conference?"

"No! It was fine. I didn't have to do anything. I signed some books. And my dad said I didn't have to wear the costume until my rash gets better." I pulled down the collar of my jacket and showed her.

"That is one nasty rash," she said.

I pulled a couple of crumpled brochures out of my pocket. "I brought you some information about the conference."

I put them on the table. Then I said the thing I had come across town to say: "I was worried when you weren't there. I haven't seen you since that time you were onstage with me." I pulled out the pen, wrapped in a paper towel; put it on the table; and said, for the third time, "I brought you something."

Mrs. M. lowered herself into the chair across from me. She touched the bundle and slowly pulled the paper off it. The pen looked especially dazzling. She smiled at me and said, quietly, "This is a pen fit for a queen."

"Everyone really missed you at the conference," I said.

One eyebrow lifted. "No need to lie, Charlie."

"Were you not invited?" I had been worried that my dad might have had something to do with her absence.

"I was invited, but I'm not going to very many conferences this year. I'm looking for a new direction." She smiled again and rubbed the top of her head.

"You're hair sure is short," I observed. "Does this mean you won't be doing any school visits either?"

"Not for a while. I'm in semiretirement. Have you been forced to do many schools lately?"

"No schools are calling. My dad is really pissed off about it. Dr. Naturo says the schools don't have any money, but we might get some action in the spring."

"Ah, the spring," Mrs. M. agreed. "Author hell."

"So I guess we're both taking a break, right Mrs. M.?"

"I guess so. A very good idea for you, my friend. Take a break. What grade are you in? Fifth? Be a fifth-grader. Make some friends."

She might as well have told me to learn to fly. Who would want to be friends with a rashy, nail-biting beetle? "Do you have any friends, Mrs. M.?"

"My very best friend died two years ago. Her name was Helen. I miss her every day."

"Wow, that makes two people that you miss. Your husband and your friend."

"That's right. Two sorely missed people. Who do you miss, Charlie?"

I was silent a moment. What a question. I skipped over the obvious answer, the biggest absence. "I miss Rita," I confessed. "She was my first babysitter. I keep a picture of her in my wallet. Want to see it?"

I had never before shown anyone my photo of Rita. It was her sixth-grade school picture; fake fireworks were exploding behind her braided head. The photo didn't do justice to her beauty, but every time I looked at it, emotions swirled inside my chest, a great longing for someone far away. Mrs. M. studied Rita's pale face for what seemed like a long time. Then she asked, "Where did she go?"

"She moved away. To Indiana with her mom. Her mom was crazy."

"What do you mean?"

"I guess she made Rita move all the time. They never stayed anywhere. That's why Rita hated her. But at least . . ." I fell silent, holding back my thought.

"At least . . . what?"

"At least I got to have her be my babysitter for a little while. Man, she was the greatest."

"And now you and your brother have a new babysitter?"

"Right."

"And how is she?"

"Julie? She's okay." The truth was that I had left Liam alone. "I should probably call Dial-a-Ride," I said. "Julie only stays until six."

"Let me make you a sandwich first," Mrs. M. said, taking charge. "And then I'll drive you home myself."

The offer astounded me. Me in a car with Mrs. M.?

"It's kind of far," I said. Also I wasn't sure I wanted her to see where I lived. But the sandwich part . . .

She stood at the nearby kitchen counter and made two ham sandwiches. "One for your brother," she explained. "In case Julie forgets to feed him."

"I think I need to eat mine right away," I said weakly. "No lettuce please."

She put one on a plate and wrapped one tightly in Saran Wrap while I watched from the table, speechless with gratitude, my stomach contracting with love.

THIRTEEN

I am in a gymnasium at a book conference, but instead of books to sell, I am selling sandwiches; there are stacks of sandwiches all around me, and everybody else is selling books. I feel conspicuous and humiliated, but I keep making the sandwiches—ham and Velveeta and mustard. I decide to yell, "Sandwiches for sale!" but the room is so noisy with teachers and authors and everybody talking at once that my voice is drowned out and nobody notices me. From across the room, I see my dad; he turns away from the woman he is talking to, and the crowd parts, and he is staring at me. Then he shakes his head very slowly at me, very slowly, while his face collapses into tears; he is so upset that I am selling sandwiches instead of books. He covers his head with his arms and starts to cross the gymnasium, stumbling and weeping. I want him to stay away. I don't want to see his tears or hear his voice or smell his breath.

"Stay back!" I command. "I'll give you all the sandwich money if you stay back!"

I wake up. I hear Clara sigh and turn over in her bed.

◆ ◆ ◆

When I was ten, there was this crazy blowout conference in Flint, Michigan, of all places—this one was called Kids in Love with Books—I'll never forget that name. Dad was really excited about the invitation and worked hard to get me involved in as many things as possible during the two-day affair. He was trying to "get my career back on track."

Somehow, for the Kids in Love with Books Conference, Dad arranged for me to be included on a six-author panel of experts about getting published. Me! The kid who had published each one of his ridiculous books on a copy machine. What advice could I have possibly given anybody that day? How to become the world's youngest published author? Have an insane dad who tells anybody who will listen to him that you're the world's youngest published author.

So there I was, sitting beside Mrs. M., also on the author panel, jiggling my knee so hard under the white tablecloth that she grabbed it and pressed it still. We were both bored. While the other real authors pontificated and explained the details of their publishing tricks, we sat in complete silence for the entire hour. Nobody asked either one of us a single question about getting published, probably because the four other authors were all being so chatty and enthusiastic. Not us. We knew the score. We were burnouts.

Afterward, we had tea and a cookie in a dark corner of the conference hotel restaurant. I was hiding from Dad, thrilled to be in a shadowy booth with Mrs. M. She seemed completely exhausted, but not as crabby as usual. "Would you be all right with not seeing me anymore at these events, Charlie?" she asked.

"Oh sure," I said. "I'm quitting too."

"I worry about you, Charlie."

"Don't worry about me," I insisted. But then asked curiously, "Why do you worry about me?"

"Well . . . I wasn't very nice to you when I first met you. I'm sure you remember those first few conferences. But you either didn't notice or didn't care. You followed me around like a little puppy."

I nodded, accepting this description of myself. "So . . . I shouldn't have done that?"

"I'm glad you were persistent, but you're missing my point. In the future, you need to seek out people who treat you with kindness. You need more kindness in your life, not crabby sarcasm."

"You could be more kind to me," I suggested.

"I am already being as kind to you as I can stand to be. How old are you now, Charlie?"

"Ten. People think I'm younger. My dad says to tell them I'm still six."

"I'm sure he does."

"I get crushes on girls sometimes, Mrs. M., but they always move away."

"Don't be discouraged. You do have a certain charm, Charlie. And you'll be handsome when you grow into your head."

I was stung. "Where are you going with this, Mrs. M.?"

"Well . . . I guess I want you to promise me that you'll seek out kindness when you have more friends. Including female friends. Choose a girl who is nice. She doesn't need to be a doormat, just a nice person. Will you promise me that, Charlie?"

I asked, anxiously, "Are you going somewhere, Mrs. M.?"

"No, Charlie. I'll be here. You know where I live." She broke into a song then, something that I had never heard her do before, something about seeing me in all the old familiar places.

"Stop it."

She didn't stop.

"You're really weird, Mrs. M."

She stopped singing and waved me away. "Go on, now," she said. "Find your dad and sell a few of your awful books."

"Oh *that's* real kind," I said.

FOURTEEN

I am standing at one of six sinks in the lavatory of my old elementary school in Hudsonville. To my horror, Mom and Liam come into the bathroom; they don't know it's me at the sink, but I know it's them. They come to either side of me to wash their hands. I am afraid to look up from my own sink. My own hands are covered with mud, and no soap will come out of my dispenser. I look at Mom's hands—they are translucent; as she washes them, they turn a deep frozen blue. I am even more afraid to look at Liam's hands. Beside me, Liam starts to sing. He sings an old lullaby of Mom's in the voice of a little girl—very creepy—he is singing "Hush, Little Baby." I look at his hands. Very bad, very, very bad idea—his hands are beetle claws, which he is cheerfully lathering as he sings. Water washes over the sides of his sink and begins to cover the floor of the lavatory, soaking my shoes.

I wake up with a start. I am on my back. My feet are dry. My hands are clean. I look at the clock. It is 4:30, on the morning of the day that Mom and Liam are—God help me—coming for tea.

***

I am sitting in a chair at the kitchen table when they arrive, and so I do not see their actual entrance or the first few moments of their time in Clara's house. I hear Clara's voice, bright, welcoming, and then I hear another woman's voice, soft, uncertain, and impossible. The voice says, "Here we are."

Here we are. After an eternity—here she is. I close my eyes and clutch the table edge, wishing I could run away. How in the world can this be happening? The voice had said "we," so I knew that Liam was there too, but so far no sound has come from him. Then he speaks, and the tone of his voice is assured, confident, and strangely like my voice, except that I never sound confident. He says, "Wow, great house, Clara." His tone is congratulatory, like they have had many previous conversations about houses.

"Thank—thank you, Liam," Clara stutters.

The china loop that is the handle of the teacup I've been clasping snaps off. One jagged edge leaves a shallow cut on my palm.

"Come on into the kitchen. Charlie and I made tea." But I hear an unfamiliar note of uncertainty in her voice; perhaps she is questioning the wisdom of the event already.

Then they appear. The hidden injury to my hand has settled me a bit. And at least I do not have to get up. I am a complete cripple today, my leg propped up on a chair. No fake hugs are possible. The three of them pause a moment in the kitchen entryway, unsure. Mom is looking at me; Liam is watching Mom. Then he is watching Clara's back; she has come into the kitchen to stand at the counter, fussing with the teapot. Then he looks directly at me. Then back at Clara.

Liam is a young man. His shoulders are broad. His hair is long and almost white-blond. He is movie-star handsome. His expression, as he watches Clara, is disbelieving.

I turn from this and catch my mother's eyes. She is still staring at me. I look away and then back, and still she stares. Her hair is sandy-colored, slightly gray in the front. She is wearing granny glasses, and she has age spots on her temples. I was not expecting her to look so much older. Would I have recognized her on the street? Finally, she turns away. I look down at my hand, clenched into a single fist on my lap. A circle of blood has bloomed on my plaid pajama leg. We are all so very, very trapped.

"Sit down, everybody," Clara instructs.

But nobody moves. Clara puts the teapot at the center of the table, steps back from the table, and giggles. "I know it's strange," she says, "but I'm so glad you guys came over. We both are."

"Strange?" Liam repeats, teasing her. It is immediately obvious that he owns the room now. "What's strange about it?" Then he laughs too, but not nervously. Intimately. Slyly.

"We were glad to be invited," Mom says. "Even if it is a bit strange. And we weren't sure how Charles would feel about it."

Then there is silence, everyone waiting for me to say I feel great about it. When this doesn't happen, Clara begins pouring tea into the four waiting cups. She notices I've broken mine but says nothing. I am still the only one seated.

Liam's voice is now thick with sympathy. "Sorry to hear you tore up your leg, Charlie. Bummer. We had no idea."

"Guess I should have called."

"Nobody is saying you should have called," Liam snaps back.

With my other thumb, I press more blood from the cut in my palm.

Clara says, "I *told* him he should call you guys, like, so many times!"

"Never mind," says Mom. "There have been many... lost opportunities. But here we are, all together today. One kitchen. Both my sons. I am very grateful for this moment." Then she looks very, very directly at me and adds, "You don't have to be glad we are here, Charles. I understand if you aren't."

At first I don't know how to respond to this. But then I decide to be honest. "Today is only possible because I can't run away."

"Oh, he's just kidding," Clara giggles. She looks desperate around the eyes.

But Mom doesn't flinch. "I'm sure that's true, Charles." she says. She takes a sip of her tea. "The tea is very nice," she says to Clara.

I sip mine too. It's too strong, very bitter. I add sugar.

Liam is having a hard time sitting still; he begins to roam the apartment, uninvited. This makes me remember what a fidgety kid he was—one of the things that got him into trouble in school. He was always "disrupting class" and "ruining quiet time." Maybe this is part of what he brings to his musical performances, the same energy that made him scamper and howl in the old apartment, desperate to be noticed by the babysitter. He comes back into the kitchen and meets my eyes, his expression challenging now. He must hate me so much. Would he try to hurt me if we were alone?

Something Clara is telling Mom makes me suddenly return my attention to them. Clara is saying something about the medical bills—not at all a safe topic. I lean forward in alarm at the table, making the teacups clatter. Everyone looks at me.

"My insurance covers everything," I say, my voice suddenly loud and insistent. "I have plenty of money, and I'm going back to work in a month or so."

None of this is true, but my urgency silences Clara.

"Where were you working?" Mom asks.

"At Bodacious Bikes. On Morton Street. They have really good insurance for all their employees." I send Clara a warning look. She gets it.

Mom nods, but I have the distinct feeling she knows that we are refusing to involve her. Liam breaks the silence again. "I really like your house, Clara. Pretty cool to have your own house. When I go to Interlochen in the fall, I'll be living in a dorm. I hope I can stand living in a small space with a bunch of other crazy musicians." He looks at me then, meaningfully. Was this his way of reminding me that he is not stuck, not a fuck-up, not a cripple?

The cheeriness has come back into Clara's voice at Liam's news. "That is so great, Liam. God, Mrs. Porter, won't you miss him?"

I cannot believe Clara has said this. It is a new high in the absurdity of the gathering. The woman who ran away from her children? A streak of cruelty surfaces in me, uncontrollable: "Yeah, won't you miss him . . . , Mom?" I echo.

Mom turns to face me. She wears her hair in a plain pony-tail with bangs, the same hairdo I remember from before I started school. She has deep creases from her outer nose to the sides of her mouth, frown lines. She is a frowner. I will probably have the same lines soon. Her eyebrows are invisible behind her glasses. But her eyes are a dark, stony blue. My eyes. She says, "Yes, I will miss him."

Oh, the things I could have said then! The dark places I could have pushed her into. Right into the dreams, where a giant beetle is waiting. But I look away and clench my jaw.

And then suddenly, appallingly, Clara chimes in with her sunniest voice, "Maybe we should have a going-away party for Liam!"

"Great idea," Liam drawls, after a beat. There is a gleam of triumph in his smile.

They leave soon after this. Liam tells Clara he has a violin lesson back in Grand Rapids. He tells her he is preparing for his big audition at Interlochen, a scholarship waiting if he does well. As they leave the apartment, I stay rooted to my chair, letting Clara handle the good-byes. My leg is throbbing; I need to move. As soon as they are gone, I lope around the apartment, flexing my uninjured leg, putting a little weight on the bad one. Clara comes back into the kitchen and watches as I do this. "Did you cut yourself?" she asks, looking at the stain on my pants.

"It's nothing," I insist.

She looks away. Perhaps it is dawning on her that I am a gloomy, prone-to-injury boyfriend with too many secrets.

◆ ◆ ◆

Before sleep that night, Clara comes to the side of the sofa bed and leans close and strokes my hair.

"Are you mad at me?" she asks.

I am, but I ask, "Why would I be mad at you?"

"I don't know. Maybe today wasn't such a great idea."

"Too late now."

"But, Charlie, didn't it go better than you expected?"

"I don't know what I expected."

"No tears anyway. No threats. Nobody screaming or swearing, right?"

"Is that what *you* expected? That one of us would start screaming? Are you disappointed? Not enough drama for you?"

She sits up. "You *are* mad at me. I knew it. Don't shut me out, Charlie! I admit it was a little strange. I felt stressed out by it too. I don't know how to make it right."

"Well, here's a start. Promise me that you will not make any further plans to see my mom or my brother without thoroughly discussing it with me first."

She said, almost too quickly, "Promise."

"No, I'm serious. Really, really promise me. No exceptions."

"I heard you, Charlie. I won't do it again. I promise." But her tone is fretful. She is disappointed in me for always being so negative. Nothing can be done about it.

◆ ◆ ◆

"I'm glad you came to my house again, Charlie, because I've been needing to tell you something. I've been invited to several author events this spring, and I said no to every single invitation. And it felt good. So I've decided that I won't be coming to any author conferences ever again. And I also think that I will enjoy what's left of my life more if I stop pretending that I'm writing something of value."

We are on Mrs. M.'s porch; she had poured us lemonade. I

sip mine. It is divine. "Are you sure, Mrs. M.?"

"I'm very sure."

I wasn't surprised. But I felt suddenly terribly sad. Perhaps my sadness showed on my anemic, rashy face.

"No moping, now," Mrs. M. said. "You can come over and visit me anytime. We'll share a glass of champagne on my front porch."

"Mrs. M.," I said. "I'm ten."

She smiled. "Why do I sometimes feel like you're the same age as me?"

I thought a moment. "Maybe because we both hate being authors together. It's our bond."

She smiled. "Right you are, Charlie. My point is that you can come over and see me any time you need to. Any time you need to escape your . . . situation."

My situation. Who else knew about it? Who else knew how difficult it was, living with the two amigos, hating them both, hating school, having no friends, and being the world's youngest and most neurotic and annoying and unloved children's book author.

"Why don't you bring that brother of yours over here sometime?" she asked. "I would very much like to meet him."

"Oh sure," I agreed. But thinking, *Never*.

The very next Saturday, I knocked on her door again. When she opened it, I said, "Any champagne left?"

This made her laugh. Mrs. M. laughed! Her laugh was an explosion of craziness. More of a bark than a laugh.

I had brought my Beetle Boy costume with me in a plastic grocery bag because I had decided that I was also going to retire. If it was making Mrs. M. happy, maybe I could get happier too.

Mrs. M. could see right away what I had brought with me—the pipe-cleaner antennae were curling out of the bag.

"Were you planning on performing for me?" she asked.

"I was planning on burning it in your fireplace."

She asked me if I'd had dinner. She said she'd made a meatloaf. I'd never had meatloaf before. That was the night of the bonfire in her alley. She thought my costume would make too much smoke for the house, so she rolled an empty metal barrel away from her garage and put in papers, kindling, and her own black cape. Then my costume. Then she went back into her house and came out with the red wig on her head and a folder of half-finished firefly stories. Everything went into the barrel. We were laughing and hollering, and one of her neighbors actually yelled out the window for us to keep it down. That made us laugh harder. When it started getting dark, she offered to take me home before somebody called the cops on us for disorderly conduct.

"I don't want to go home," I said. "I'll have to tell my dad I don't have a costume anymore. He'll kill me."

Then there was a long silence—no more laughing. "Does your father ever hurt you, Charlie?" Mrs. M. asked. "You need to tell me if he does."

"He doesn't hit me," I said, and it was true. I wasn't counting the yanking and pushing and grabbing. Or the names he called me—*idiot*, *retard*, *pussy*. "He just gets me to do whatever he wants because . . . because . . . he just gets people to do what he wants. I can't explain it. He just always has crazy ideas, and we have to go along with them. That's how it's always been."

"But you are planning to tell him that you won't be Beetle Boy anymore, right?"

I shrugged. I was suddenly feeling a deep sense of defeat. What was I thinking? "Maybe I'll just tell him I lost the costume."

She shook her head, disagreeing. "He'll get someone to make you another one, Charlie. You know that. You're going to have to be more clear than that."

"I hardly get any jobs anymore anyway," I said. "Dad says I'm getting too old, and it's spoiling the effect."

She listened with grave concern. "It sounds like you're just hoping that the whole Beetle Boy thing will just go away by itself."

I nodded. It honestly did seem vaguely possible. Because of my size. Because of my actual age. Because my voice was changing. Because I wasn't cute anymore.

"You're forgetting someone," Mrs. M. said.

I didn't answer.

"Charlie, you're forgetting someone."

"Can we just . . . can we please talk about it some other time?" I asked. "I think I'm getting sick from inhaling fumes." We had been laughing only a few moments ago, but now I was feeling a terrible burden. "Can you please drive me home?" I asked.

She looked away, shaking her head. We walked back into her house in silence. "Get your jacket," she said. "It's in the front hallway."

She made a meatloaf sandwich for Liam and drove me back to Grove Street. Before I got out of the car, with the sandwich in my pocket, she said, "Will you come back and see me whenever you need to?"

"Right, Mrs. M.," I said numbly.

"And one of these times, will you bring your brother?"

"Okeydokey," I agreed. I was under such a black cloud of dread and guilt that I wasn't sure I'd ever see her again myself. It was that bad.

FIFTEEN

It is early, the morning after the big visit, and Clara has come to my bed to wake me. She is excited about something, and I am having trouble waking up after a long night of tossing and turning.

"Rise and shine, Charlie," she says. "Are you getting excited about where we're going today?" She pounds my chest and belly lightly, determined to get me moving.

"Stop it."

"Are you forgetting you might get some good news today?"

"There is no good news in the forecast."

"Charlie! Remember what today is?"

"Don't you have to go to work soon?"

"It's my day off, remember? I took today off because of your big doctor's appointment."

She is right. This is why she is excited. It could possibly be the day they remove my cast and replace it with the walking boot. Remembering this, I feel a fluttering of excitement too at the prospect of no more cast and being able to walk without crutches. I smile at Clara hopefully, thankful that she kept track of my appointment, but she doesn't return my smile.

"Charlie, please tell me why you moved your boxes out of my closet."

I hadn't thought she would notice—at least not right away. I had underestimated her yet again. I decide in a flash to give her an answer, albeit a dishonest one.

"I thought they might be taking up too much room."

"Oh, really? Really, Charlie? Your few little boxes taking up too much room in my big old closet? How considerate of you. Where did you move them to, Charlie?"

I meet her eyes. I so completely do not want to tell her where I put the boxes that for a long moment, I can't speak at all. My tongue is paralyzed. I shake my head, trying to communicate wordlessly how impossible it is for me to tell her where the boxes are. She attacks from a new direction.

"Tell me more about that cousin who died."

Oh God. The damn cousin who died. An old lie, coming back to bite my ass. I don't want to add to it. I take a deep breath. "Not my cousin," I say. "Don't know why I said it was a cousin. Just a girl I knew. Someone. From a long time ago, nobody important."

She is rightly bewildered. "So did the girl actually die?"

Another long pause. "No. She just . . . went away. Look, I don't know why I said she died. I felt embarrassed. I didn't want to have to explain why I still have her stupid picture."

"Why *do* you still have her stupid picture?"

"There's no reason. There's nothing to tell. It meant something to me once. I guess I loved her. I don't know. She was my babysitter. I was like seven years old." I add, pleadingly, "I had a really fucked-up childhood, okay? You've figured that much out, haven't you?"

She nods. "I feel so sad for you right now."

"Don't say that. Please. Don't feel sad for me. Please. I can't stand having people feel sad for me."

"But everything I learn about you is sad, Charlie. Every single thing."

"That's not true. You just think that because you had a happy childhood. It's no big deal, Clara. Quit making it so hard. Lots of people are like me."

Now a longer pause. Clara is recalculating her opinion of me. I can actually see it happening in her eyes. Finally, she speaks. Her voice is cold. "So I'm the one making things hard, is that it?"

"I didn't mean it the way it sounded."

"Where did you put the boxes, Charlie?"

I swallow hard. "They're in the garage. Behind some old vases. Please, could you just leave them there for now?"

"We have to get ready to go to the doctor's. We should leave in about half an hour. But first, I want you to bring me that picture. The one I already saw. Of the little girl who didn't die."

She is looking hard at me, harder than ever before. But I look back at her, and I am hard too. It feels like a standoff. It feels like something where one of us has to give in. Me. I ask, "If I do, will you promise to leave my boxes alone?"

It sounds so stupid! *Leave my boxes alone.* It sounds like we are in preschool! I could almost start laughing, it sounds so stupid. But I am completely serious. And so is she.

"I promise to leave your boxes alone if you bring me that picture."

So I go out to the garage and move the vases and pull one of the boxes off the shelf and open it. I come back into the kitchen, where Clara is waiting, and I hand her the tiny, pathetic, ridiculous picture. She takes it from my hand, looks at it a moment, and then fastens Rita to the fridge with a magnet.

"Why are you putting her on the fridge?" I ask.

"Because it's something real about you."

Something real about me. I guess that's true—Rita was real. She's not something I dreamed or invented or stole. "We better hurry," I say. "I don't want to be late for my appointment."

"We won't be late. I'll be ready in ten minutes. Just please don't lie to me about your childhood anymore."

"Okay," I say.

◆ ◆ ◆

I went six years without going back to Mrs. M.'s house. Why? Was it because I was mad at her for being so concerned about Liam? Was it because I had to do three final author gigs without a costume? Did I blame her? Did I feel abandoned? I don't know. I just let it get away from me. I think, in some ways, I made this decision not to think any more about her. Not to need her. She became another woman I refused to need.

The first year, my first year in middle school, was a terrible time for me because even though there were basically no more author jobs, Dad was still moving full speed ahead with new Beetle Boy books—the final two. These books were, if it's even possible, the worst ones we had done. Sam Church was no longer interested in illustrating them, and it showed. He had never been paid for the previous two books, and some of the drawings looked like he had forgotten to finish them—Beetle Boy often appeared without antennae or missing his spots or his eyeballs. And unlike the first set, there was basically no background— they were just dead bugs on a blank page. I'm no artist, but even at age eleven, I could see that they were bad. But Dad was still operating on blind ambition, refusing to give up his dream of easy money on the author circuit, probably because he had no idea what he would do instead.

Ever since I burned the costume (I told him I lost it), he must have sensed that his days of manipulating me were numbered; I was building up the courage to defy him completely.

Everything came to a whimpering halt one afternoon at a school book fair in Nunica, where I was the featured guest author. There was no fee, so the gig depended entirely on book sales, a surefire disaster since the new books were so lame and I was surrounded by real books at lower prices. That day Dad was openly angry at me, a new and barely controlled anger that was obvious to everybody from the way he glared at me, dragged me by the elbow into the school library, pushed me into the book signing chair, and then stormed out of the room. In the car afterward, he threw several books at my head, one at a time.

Dad was losing it. He was losing his charm. He was losing his looks—getting bald, getting paunchy. He was way less successful with women. His dad still sent him a check from time to time, but he basically had no other income.

But there was one thing he still had—another son. A younger, cuter, smarter, and completely available son. Once he shifted his focus onto Liam, I was off the hook. Or, I should say, I was off the hook for author gigs. I was still hanging by my neck off a big meat hook of guilt, another reason I couldn't face Mrs. M.

I was now in seventh grade. Perhaps because I wasn't ugly or obnoxious, I was pretty much left alone by my peers. I was a loner. None of the teachers at the middle school knew I had ever been Beetle Boy—not that it would have impressed them. Nothing else about me stood out. I was quiet. I sat in the back. I was medium-sized with no physical presence. I got Bs and Cs, and nobody was checking my report card. I drifted from seventh grade to eighth grade to ninth grade in a lonely fog.

Dad started making Liam do the author visits. He did two or three of them a month, a fact I tried hard to ignore, since it was pretty obvious he hated doing it just as much as I had. Right around that time, Ruby started in as our babysitter. It was Liam who found Ruby; she lived with her grandmother in Green Grove No. 15. At first she ignored me and I ignored her—I thought I was way past caring about babysitters. She ignored Liam too. She had more mature tastes.

The months passed. The years passed. During those years I did not miss Mrs. M. because I could not imagine myself back in touch with her. I wasn't a child anymore. I couldn't approach her like a child; I knew better. Meanwhile, in our apartment, life was turning into a bad made-for-TV movie, and I was feeling more and more like I had to get away.

The lost years. Before I found within myself the initiative to make a deal with my old friend, the only person I knew who could get me out of my new hell.

◆ ◆ ◆

We are at the Grandville Surgical Clinic and I have had an amazingly successful appointment and I am minus my cast and have been properly fitted for a walking boot and I am actually walking in it. We are both thrilled, and so there is no stopping Clara from approaching the billing and insurance station and taking on the issue of my surely astronomical and overdue medical bills, which I have been avoiding.

"Hello, I'm Clara and this is Charlie Porter and he is a patient here and we'd like to set up a payment plan for his medical bills."

As if any sort of payment plan was remotely possible.

The medical receptionist is elderly and finds my file after a slow search and a lot of frowning. Then she squints past Clara, looking at me. "You are Charles Allen Porter?"

I nod, bracing for the news that I will be sent to debtor's prison.

"You're all paid up, Mr. Porter," she says. "Nothing currently due."

Clara and I exchange glances.

"But, ma'am, ma'am," Clara sputters, "We haven't actually paid for anything yet. We never even got any bills."

The receptionist glances at the page again. "Your balance was forwarded by request to a Mrs. Martha Manning in Cedar Rapids, Iowa. Your grandmother."

"His grandmother?"

"O-KAY!" I jump in, needing to quickly get us both out of the building. "Okay, keep us posted, thanks so much!"

I take Clara's arm and lead her away as best I can with my new, crutch-free gait, the walking boot clunking noisily on the tiled floors of the building. Clara is silent, scowling in deep thought, letting me pull her along, until we are out of the clinic and in the parking lot. Then she shakes her arm free. "Excuse me! EXCUSE me! You have a grandmother who pays your bills? And you never once mentioned it?"

"She's not my grandmother. Honestly, Clara, she's not."

"Then who is Martha Manning?"

"She's a friend," I say. "She's old and she was really sick and I didn't know . . . I didn't know . . . I thought she was dead."

"Oh, here we go again. Somebody else conveniently dead."

"No, seriously. Because she was really sick the last time I saw her. And then later I found out she was dying."

"Well, apparently she's alive enough to be paying all your medical bills! Which is kinda strange, if you ask me. What is this all about?"

"I don't know. I don't know. It's . . . unbelievable!"

"Is she superrich, this Mrs. Manning? And how did she even know about your injury?"

"I have no clue! She moved to Iowa a year ago. To her sister's. Her sister was going to help her . . . you know . . . die." I stop walking. I wrap my arms around my head. "But she didn't die," I groan. "She's not dead."

"Oh my God, are you upset? Oh, Charlie, you're really upset."

Clara has never seen me cry. She is stunned, silent for the rest of the walk to the car, the rest of the drive to her apartment. When we are parked beside her house, she comes around to the passenger side to help me. "Can you get out of the car okay with the boot, Charlie? Do you need a crutch to lean on?"

"No, I'm okay. Just let me go slow."

She steps back. I get out, awkwardly, and she takes my arm.

"Look at you! No more crutches! No overdue bills! And your old friend isn't dead. This is a good day, isn't it, Charlie?"

"It is." I am weak—my other leg is already sore but stable. Clara stays close. I reach for her and pull her close and kiss the top of her head hard, trembling with gratitude, tearing up again. She is still with me. I look around the driveway. I am here. I am okay. I am Charlie Porter without crutches, without bills, and with my girlfriend by my side. Someone who was dead is not dead. I am blinking in amazement at the bright sun.

SIXTEEN

I am in Mrs. M.'s kitchen, waiting for her to wake up and have her coffee. I've put her cup of coffee on her placemat at the breakfast nook, from where she will be able to watch the birds. I hear the sound of her getting up, and I look proudly at the cup I've prepared for her, when to my horror, I see a large, black disconnected claw resting at the edge of the table. I pick up the claw—it's hard and shiny and surprisingly heavy. Mrs. M. enters the kitchen in her purple robe and her wig and she finds me holding the claw.

"I keep finding them around the house," she says. "It looks like we're pretty badly infested. Do you know how to get rid of them?"

"No," I say. I throw the claw into Mrs. M.'s open garbage canister, noticing that there are half a dozen shiny claws already in the bottom of the bag.

◆ ◆ ◆

I come out of the bathroom, after a shower that includes standing briefly with my weight on both legs, a hamstring stretch under the hot spray, and brief, expert masturbating. A great shower. I am in the best mood I've been in for a long time, and I wander shirtless into the kitchen in my sweatpants with one leg cut out to fit over my boot. And there I find my brother, Liam, sitting at the kitchen table, with—I kid you not—Clara's teapot and a fucking cup of tea.

"Liam—Jesus! How did you get in here?"

"Window," he says. He points to Clara's open kitchen window. The screen is leaning against the wall beneath it. The windowsill is dirty from his shoes. He is wearing black jeans and a T-shirt that says Fear the Violins. He grins at me, proud of himself.

"You . . . you can't do that, Liam!" I sputter. "This is Clara's house. Jesus, we have a door. What happened to knocking on the door?"

"I did knock on the door. I thought you might be asleep. I decided to come in anyway. I took a chance you might be happy to see me when you woke up."

"*Jesus*, Liam!"

"What, you aren't happy to see me?"

"Hell, no, I'm not happy to see you because you fucking broke into my girlfriend's house, Liam!"

He shrugs. "If you want, I can go back outside and knock on your door and you can open the door and say, 'Little Brother! What a pleasant surprise!'"

"Liam, what are you *doing* here?"

"But you wouldn't say that, would you, Charlie. It's not a pleasant surprise to see me, is it? I saw the way you looked at us when we were here."

"How did you get all the way over here by yourself? Did you drive?"

"I can't drive by myself yet. I rode my bike. Took me a

couple of hours. I'm in great physical shape, in case you haven't noticed. And I can totally chill about school now. Did you hear I won first place at that audition last week?"

I close my eyes and speak through my teeth. "That's really great. Way to go."

He scoffs. "You don't give a rip. Don't pretend you do. You probably can't believe I'm good at anything, right? Since I wasn't so good at being you."

He has caught me off guard. I don't know what to say in reply. I rub the back of my head and say, "It was a bad situation."

"A bad situation. Yeah, that's one way to put it." A long pause. Then, "Have a seat." He points to the chair across from him.

But I don't want to sit down. Sitting down means a conversation. Sitting down means looking him in the eye. I remain standing and ask, "Did you come all the way over here just to tell me you won the audition?"

"No. I was thinking maybe we could talk about Mom. She's gonna be by herself when I go to Interlochen. Sometimes I feel bad about that. She's still such a loner."

Now, I do sit down. I need to make myself very clear. I say, "Liam, this is the first time we've had a conversation in how long?"

"Two years."

I note the fact that he has kept track. "Let me get this out there right now. I am not interested in having any sort of relationship with Mom. Now or ever. Seeing her the other day made that all the more clear. You need to just accept that."

"Oh, I need to accept it? Really? Why do I have to accept that? Because you're older than me? Because you have things all figured out?" He is smiling when he says this, and it is a dazzling smile. But menacing.

"Liam, I'm trying to tell you how it is with me."

"Hey, maybe we could talk instead about that old lady who let you live at her house. That was sure nice of her. I showed the house to Mom on our way back from having tea with you and Clara. It had a For Sale sign on the front lawn. It looked empty."

The idea of them doing this—checking out Mrs. M.'s house—makes me suddenly nauseous with guilt.

"What was her name anyway? Was she some kind of teacher?"

"Her name was Martha. She wasn't a teacher. She doesn't live around here anymore."

"Mom said she wished she could have met her. Not me, though. She never did shit for me."

I think then of all the sandwiches and snacks that Mrs. M. gave me for Liam, none of which he ever saw. Of how she always asked questions about him, none of which he ever heard. The kitchen seems suddenly darker, full of trouble, a storm settling over us. I say softly, "Liam, God, I just really had to get away from Dad."

"Oh, right. Right. *You* had to get away." A pause. "I didn't even write those books, *Charlie*. You wrote them. But I had to lie all the *time* and say I wrote them. Dad told me my professional name was Charlie."

"Look, Liam, I couldn't help it that Dad made you do that. You know I couldn't help it. It was every man for himself with Dad."

Liam is staring out the window in the kitchen now, and he says without turning around, "The thing I hated most was that

I had to say I was you. That was worse than having to recite those idiotic stories."

Is he about to cry? I'm not sure. I stand up again, in alarm. I feel sick to my stomach at the thought of witnessing Liam's tears. But he turns back to me, and his expression is almost cheerful.

"Matter of fact, I had somebody who helped me too. I mean, before Mom came back for me. My fifth-grade music teacher, Mrs. Davis. She got me a violin and paid for my lessons. She saw right away that I had talent."

"I'm glad someone helped you too," I say, with some urgency because I really mean it. It seems like a way that we can reconnect.

Liam takes a noisy slurp of tea. "Your girlfriend is *hot*," he reports.

I flinch but say nothing.

"No girlfriends for me right now. Not that I don't have girls interested. Especially older girls. I guess you know what I mean." He laughs, a strange, brittle sound—it occurs to me that I have never heard this adult-Liam laugh. There is a familiar meanness in it. I resist the impulse to cover my ears.

Liam is watching me, reading my thoughts. "Ever hear from Dad?" he asks.

I shake my head. "You?"

"Oh God, no. No idea where he is, but he's not allowed to come anywhere near me. Mom put a restraining order on him because of the whole Ruby thing. It got pretty insane. You missed all the fun. Lucky you, right?"

I desperately want him to leave now. Does he sense it? I meet his eyes; they are a hard, bright blue under thick white-blond eyebrows—Dad's eyes. Then he takes a final slurp of tea and stands up and looks around the kitchen one more time. Something catches his eye on the refrigerator. "Why do you have a picture of Rita Dean on your refrigerator?"

"You remember Rita?"

"Course I remember her. She was the worst babysitter we ever had. She was a total bitch to me."

"She was just a kid, Liam. Just a kid in a bad situation, like us."

He looked at me, his eyes round, as though he couldn't believe his ears. "Whoa. Is that why you have her picture on your refrigerator? To remind you of what a super-concerned person you are about people caught in bad situations? Holy crap. Keep telling yourself that, Charlie."

He strolls out of the kitchen. I hear him pause at the front door. "See you around," he calls. The door slams. When I go into the living room to make sure he is gone, I see a scrap of paper on the floor. Shit. Shit. It's an old note in my own handwriting. Liam has left it on the floor for me. The same note I left on the floor for him, the day I moved out of Green Grove, leaving him behind.

◆ ◆ ◆

There were no slammed doors that day; mine was a stealth departure. I basically didn't take anything with me; I had a trash bag full of clothes and a box of books and papers for school, and that was it. No prolonged and visible moving out. By that time, I was used to coming in and out of the apartment without anyone talking to me. It was a Saturday. Liam was there, still in bed. Dad was in the kitchen with Ruby.

I heard them talking in low voices. "You would love Jamaica," Dad is telling her. "I have to figure out a way that we could all live down there."

Ruby's voice, breathless with excitement. "Would your dad really let us all live with him? You said his house is huge. Wouldn't that be so cool?"

A big house was unlikely, but I was not surprised that Dad had told her this. He was always talking big about hitting up rich Grandpa Ned. Liam and I barely listened anymore—neither of us had ever met the man—but Ruby was a novice. She added, still breathless, "Won't he disapprove of our relationship, Dan?"

"He can kiss my ass," Dad growled, suddenly angry. "It's about time he did something for me."

"I don't want to go if he won't approve of me," Ruby complained. "I get enough of that from everybody else around here. Especially Charlie. He looks at me like I'm some kind of monster-girl." This was a lie. I made a point never to look at her. She started to cry. I heard him taking her in his arms, their pajamas rustling. He said, comforting her, "Charlie's an idiot."

I had an impulse before I left—a guilt impulse that I couldn't ignore. I felt compelled to say something to Liam. Something that would help him to make sense of having no more brother. So I wrote him a note. A pathetic little note, not a real explanation or a real good-bye. Just a few stupid sentences in my terrible handwriting: *I found a better place to live. Dad doesn't hate you as much as he hates me. I'll be seeing you. Good luck. Charlie*

◆ ◆ ◆

I am so happy to see Clara when she gets home from work that I almost break into a run to greet her at the door. I stop myself, remembering that I can't run yet. She opens the door, sees me grimacing, and thinks something new is wrong with me.

"What is it, Charlie?" she cries. "Did you have a fall?"

"No, I'm good. I was moving a little too fast because I was just . . . I'm just so glad to see you, that's all. C'mere."

She is carrying a plastic bag of groceries, and she sets it down and comes close and lets me hug her. "Was it a good day? Do you want to take a little walk?"

"Let's take a drive," I say. "I want to show you something."

"Really? Something important?"

"Something important."

"Okay, great. Just let me put these few groceries away. Then we'll go. But, Charlie, I don't think you should drive yet."

"I want you to drive. I want to talk. I want to show you where I was living last year."

"I've seen the motel, remember? I moved you out of it."

"No, before that. When I lived with Mrs. M."

"You mean . . . Martha Manning?" she asks, thrilled. "Her house? Will we be able to go inside?"

I don't answer this question. I am thinking I'll decide what to do when we get there.

SEVENTEEN

Clara and I are standing beside the For Sale sign in front of Mrs. M.'s single-story ranch house. The windows are dark; the green exterior is freshly painted; there are still two white Adirondack chairs on the porch—our chairs. I have not been in this neighborhood since the day I ruptured my Achilles tendon running away from what I had learned inside the house, collapsing curbside into a puddle of mush. Mrs. M.'s next-door neighbor saw me fall and called 911 on his cell phone; he kept calling me Chris and telling me to calm down. I was trying to get up, but I couldn't get my leg to stop screaming. I think I also might have been screaming, literally, just a little, until an ambulance came and two guys put me on a gurney. I remember telling the doctor in the emergency room that I am apparently a person who is not supposed to run, ever. He said, "Now, now, this could have happened to anyone."

Wrong. It could have only happened to me. On that day, in that neighborhood, in that terribly public way, it could only have happened to me because I am Charlie Porter. Something good was happening to me (Clara), and balance was needed quickly. When I entered Mrs. M.'s house, after she was long gone, I got my comeuppance.

The realtor's sign says, "Recently Reduced." I am glad the house hasn't sold yet, glad it is technically still the house I briefly shared with Mrs. M. I find myself watching the living room picture window for movement, the shadow of a woman in a purple bathrobe crossing the room to greet me at the door.

"It looks nice, Charlie. I wish I could see the inside. At least the little room where you slept."

"It was in the basement."

"Oh no—really? Was it okay for you, living in somebody's basement?"

I reply with a sigh, "It was wonderful."

She studies my face to see if I am being sarcastic. "At least it wasn't a motel room," she says. "I couldn't believe you actually lived in a motel. That was like a place where a criminal would live."

I had gone to a lot of trouble to keep her from seeing the motel, constantly avoiding the subject of my address, always meeting her after work or on the doorstep of her house. In fact, nobody else in my life ever saw the Grand Stand Motel, room 11, home, sweet home of Charlie Porter, moving on up in the world.

But eventually there came the fateful day, the day after my outpatient surgery, when Clara had to drive me to the motel and help me gather up my stuff so I could convalesce at her house. It was a defining moment for us, the first indication that I was not the normal eighteen-year-old male I had earlier pretended to be. She already knew I had no functioning parents. That was confusing enough for her. But living in Grand Stand Motel, room 11?

I was in the car, still pretty out of it from the anesthesia, and I watched her unlock the door, push it open, and take in the sight of my room. Even without being able to see her face, I could tell she was freaked out; she stayed frozen in the doorframe and kept her hand on the knob. I managed to get out of the car and move past her on my shiny-new metal crutches.

"I'm good. I'm good. I'll take over from here," I said.

Most of my clothes were still in a plastic trash bag—very convenient. In the bathroom, I rounded up my shaving supplies, my toothbrush, and a bottle of generic shampoo. I was in a phase of reading murder mysteries from a used bookstore; a small stack of them was beside the bed—I tossed them into the plastic bag. I took my bike lock—my bike was at the shop. The laptop Mrs. M. had given me, a dead cell phone, an iPod, and half a dozen cords and chargers. These went into my raggedy backpack. Three small lidded boxes of mementos—those I would keep on my lap. The whole process took about ten minutes. I was leaving behind my dirty bedding, my faded towels, a few food items, my biking magazines, and my generally miserable single life.

"All set," I said, keeping my voice normal with a huge effort, "Wow, I'm really going to need a nap soon."

I left the key in the room, put my few belongings and my crutches in the back of her car, and somehow got myself back in on the passenger side with my three boxes. Clara was still standing frozen at the door to number 11. Maybe it was dawning on her that she would be seriously taking care of me for a while and she didn't even know me. I could be a vagrant. I could be a pathological liar. I could be a murderer. Well, the first two were right.

As we drove back to her house in silence, I was actually feeling sorry for her. She was understandably upset. She was in over her head with Charlie. My leg was starting to throb, the first inkling of the pain I was in for in the nights ahead.

"Say something, Clara," I said.

She asked me why I lived in a motel.

"I'm saving money to buy a condo," I said. She didn't laugh. Not even nervously. I remember that she said something worriedly about me not owning a suitcase.

"I have a backpack," I had replied. I was clutching the stacked boxes to my chest, wincing in pain. "I travel light."

◆ ◆ ◆

Now, in front of Mrs. M.'s deserted house, I am remembering that strange day, that first openly worried expression, the slightly panicky remark about the suitcase. I look down at Clara, who is still staring at the front of Mrs. M.'s empty house. I think, *Why didn't you call it quits after you found out I lived in a motel? Was it because of the accident? Did you feel too sorry for me to ditch me? But I'm okay now. Why are you still helping me?*

Clara looks up at me, tipping her face. "Charlie, why did Martha Manning help you?"

Her question startles me—the coincidence—and I stammer, "I guess . . . I guess . . . she couldn't resist me."

My answer disappoints her. But she is still excited to be at Martha Manning's house. "I just *really* wish I could see the inside!"

I am hesitating. The key to the back door is in my wallet. Abruptly, I leave Clara's side and start to walk along the paved driveway that runs along one side of the house. Clara follows me. I unlock my private entrance and silently lead Clara into the mudroom of the house. Then into the kitchen. The house's total emptiness silences us for a moment; our footsteps are thunderous in the hot, airless rooms. Finally, Clara speaks. "Charlie, where's all her furniture?"

"In storage. Actually, her neighbor took care of the furniture for her after she left. He's acting as her realtor."

"So where were you when this was all happening?"

"I had already moved out. I left in a huff, actually, the summer after I graduated. I was so mad at her for deciding to leave. I thought it was inconvenient and unfair. I didn't know how sick she was; she didn't tell me."

We descend the basement stairs. There is nothing to see in my old bedroom but a bare mattress on a metal frame. It looks pathetic, and Clara puts an arm around my waist, sympathetic.

"No, I really liked living down here," I insist. "It was the best year of my entire life."

I know I should add, "Besides living with you." But I can't.

Back in the kitchen, I show her the breakfast nook, the bolted window, and the bird feeders—no feed in them, no birds. The cupboards are empty. The major appliances are unplugged. The counters are blank.

In the living room, there is one solitary piece of furniture in the middle of the room. It had originally been in her small office, a room she spent very little time in during the year I lived with her. The movers had left it behind in a place of prominence. It is a beautifully carved, ornate desk—kind of

Asian-looking—and huge. Like two people could comfortably work at it. Maybe three. The top of the desk is leather. There is a note sitting there, addressed to me in her unmistakable cursive: *for Charlie Porter.*

I lead Clara to the desk. I want her to read the note. It explains many things. She picks it up and puts it close to her nose; the room is dark, and she is slightly nearsighted. She reads it out loud.

> *Charlie, I want you to have this desk. It's the only piece of furniture I own with any real value. I want you to know that I have bone cancer. My prognosis is two months without treatment. I may already be dead when you read this. I am sorry that I had to leave you so suddenly. You have certainly had too many people leave you in your short life. Don't be afraid to face the unfairness of this. You are a survivor, and you will be okay. Love, M.M.*

Clara puts the note back down on the desk and gasps loudly. "But wait, Charlie," she asks, "how did she know you'd come back to her house and read this note?"

"I don't know. It sat right here on this desk for over six months."

"So when *did* you find it?"

"The day of my accident. I read it and ran for the hills. But I didn't get far. I fell into the street right over there." I pointed to the street through the picture window.

"Oh my God. That was the day? And then you called me from the hospital."

"And you came right away."

"Oh, Charlie. What a terrible letter. But she's not dead. And now she's giving you her desk. That's so nice of her. But how in the world are we going to get it out of here?"

"I'm not sure I want it."

"Leave it to me. I'll get it out of here for you. I'll ask my dad to help."

"No, please, don't ask your dad."

"Charlie, my dad loves it when I ask for help. Any sort of help. And he has a truck. Which reminds me—he wants to take us all out to dinner soon. Can you handle another meeting with my parents now that you're feeling better?"

I groan. Clara's cell phone rings in that moment, and she looks at the number and her face clouds.

"Is it your dad?"

"No, it's somebody else. Nothing important." She slips the phone back into the front pocket of her jeans. "Thank you for bringing me here today, Charlie. Really. Thank you. And for finally telling me about your friend."

I am proud of myself for finally confiding in her. For showing her the note that had nearly destroyed me. The outing was unprompted by her, and so it seems like something of a turning point. I did it. I chose to tell her. I can tell her things, and she will not run away. I take her hand out of her pocket and hold it a moment and then bring it to my lips. My girlfriend is kind and beautiful. I whisper, "You're welcome."

◆ ◆ ◆

Back at the house, we are having a cold pizza lunch and Clara has grown quiet. For once, I actually ask her what she's thinking about.

"Well . . . I was wondering how you went about asking Martha Manning if you could live with her. That's kind of a big thing to ask a person who's not even related to you."

"I know. Actually, I made up a contract. A list of all the things that I would do for her in exchange for that room in her basement. I still have the contract."

"Don't tell me. Is it in one of your boxes?"

I go to the garage and find the right box and untie the string and lift the lid and take out the contract, rolled into a tube, typed and printed long ago on Dad's dinosaur computer. I bring it back to the kitchen table, and Clara reads it with a little smile.

It reads thus:

Dear Mrs. M.,

In exchange for letting me live at your house for 9 months and telling people that you are my grandmother, I hereby swear to

1. *Take out your trash as often as needed.*

2. *Shovel your porch and sidewalk through the winter months.*

3. *Do all yard work.*

4. *Do all your grocery shopping.*

5. *Be your driver during nonschool hours.*

6. *Sleep in your empty basement room.*

7. *Have no friend or girlfriends over. [Easy—no friends, no girlfriends.]*

8. *Never disturb you while you are writing. [Easy, she didn't write anymore.]*

9. *Never enter your upstairs bathroom. [Unnecessary, toilet and shower in the basement.]*

10. *Be out of your place no later than May 31, end of senior year. No exceptions.*

"Geez, I see what you mean about making yourself irresistible."

"I don't know why I kept it. Maybe because she signed it with that big swirly signature like that. With her diamond pen."

"Her what?"

"Oh . . . she had a special pen . . . I bought it for her. I still have that, too. She left it on the desk on the top of the note. I put it in my jacket pocket before I broke into a run."

"Can I see it?"

"It's in a different box. It's just a pen."

"Charlie?"

I head back to the garage and come back with the pen, but now I am uncomfortable, remembering the nine-year-old me who had bought the pen, remembering why I bought it—the near-hallucinatory state of gratitude I had been in at the time. Buying that pen for Mrs. M. was such a huge deal for me. It wasn't just a thank-you gift. I think I was asking her to please keep helping me. To keep *me*.

The sight of the pen makes Clara laugh. "Wow, pretty fancy-schmancy, Charlie! Diamonds! You never bought me anything with diamonds."

"I haven't been able to do much shopping lately."

"Good excuse, right? But there's something else I've been wanting to ask you about. It's not about Mrs. M. It's about your books. What in the world happened to all those cute books you wrote?"

"Clara, I don't know and I don't care."

"Come on! They must have meant something to you at the time, even if you don't care about them anymore. They were your very own creation, Charlie! You were an author! I'd love to see them. Does Liam have them?"

"I don't know."

"Can I ask him?"

"I would prefer that you don't talk to Liam, Clara. Like, ever."

"But, Charlie, what if he calls me?"

"Why would he call you?"

"I don't know. Just . . . it would be awkward. I would have to say *something*."

"No, you wouldn't. If he ever calls you, you just hand over the phone to me. I deal with Liam."

She rolls her eyes. "Whatever, Charlie. But ask him if he has any of your old books, okay?"

Oh sure, I agree silently. *I'll ask him the next time he breaks in.*

◆ ◆ ◆

I am in Clara's bed, surrounded by Clara's popsicle-colored underpants, but instead of Clara beside me, Liam is sleeping on his back, with his violin resting on his chest. I am afraid to move because I don't want to wake him up, I don't want him to see Clara's underpants and ask me about them. I keep very still, until something catches my eye. Something is moving around inside of Liam's violin; something is making the wood pulse and strain. I watch in alarm

127

as a small, black, probing leg comes out of the S-shaped sound hole. I realize that Liam has a large bug inside of his violin. But it can't get out—the sound holes are too narrow. I wonder if he knows. I wonder if I should tell him. I wonder if it is partly why he plays the violin so well. I lift myself onto one elbow to ask him, but he cringes in his sleep and recoils from me, wrapping his arms tightly around his violin. "Liam," I say, "there's something I need to tell you about your violin!"

"Charlie!" Clara barks. "You're talking in your sleep again. Stop it!"

I had fallen asleep in her bed after unusually successful sex. But the dreams came anyway, following me into Clara's bed, making sure I don't forget to bring my beetle friends to the party. "Sorry, sorry, sorry, Clara. At least no screaming this time, right?"

"Shut UP! I have to go to work early tomorrow."

"Don't kick me out," I murmur. I'm pretty sure she won't. She is too nice. But I think to myself before I fall back to sleep, *Definitely not as nice as she used to be.*

EIGHTEEN

Clara is gone, and I look at the clock. I have slept in until nearly ten. Usually Clara wakes me to have breakfast with her. Then I remember that she said something in the middle of the night about going in early. She has let me sleep in. I get up and see that she has put bread and cereal on the counter for me. Coffee in a thermos. She still loves me. I eat the breakfast she has left for me and let the memories come.

◆ ◆ ◆

I am back in Mrs. M.'s neighborhood after six years of not seeing her, ringing her doorbell. At first she didn't recognize me. She asked, "Can I help you?" in a puzzled voice, keeping the screen door locked.

I waited for her to figure out that it was me. I noticed that her gray hair had grown out into curls around her face and was actually kind of pretty for an old person's hair. I asked, helpfully, "Read any good bug books lately?"

She said, "Charlie Porter, as I live and breathe." She unlocked the screen door and opened it wide. I had already decided that I was going to ask her if I could live in her basement, but I had promised myself I wouldn't bring it up that first visit. Didn't want to overwhelm her. Instead, I followed her into her kitchen, where I sat down and told her that I was sorry that I hadn't come over in six years.

"My life got complicated."

"Everybody's life is complicated," Mrs. M. said. "Your life was insane."

I asked her something I had sometimes wondered during those six years. "Did you ever wonder how I was doing?"

"Of course," she said. "Routinely. Are you still living in the apartment on Grove Street?"

"Same sitch, no improvements."

"Well . . . I saw something in the paper a couple of years ago that deeply concerned me, Charlie. I almost called you. It was a bookstore ad for a book signing—a talented young author named Charlie Porter was signing his books at the new children's bookstore in Grandville. With a photograph of a boy who clearly wasn't you."

"Yeah, I know. Guess who got the job after I quit?"

"As I feared he would. And he actually had to tell people he was you? Nice. So is he still doing Charlie Porter author events?"

"No. He's thirteen now; he's too old. But he didn't seem to mind it as much as me. He doesn't come back from the author gigs and cry on his bed for an hour like I used to. Or get hives. Or have panic attacks. But we actually never talk about it. We don't talk in my family. We don't share."

A silence. Mrs. M. asked me if I was hungry, which I was.

"You've grown taller than I would have expected," she said. "You were small for your age."

"I grew into my head," I said, a comment I had never forgotten.

She chuckled, remembering it too. "And no scars from all those rashes on your neck. That's good. What grade are you in now?"

"I'm sixteen, but I'm heading into my senior year. I started school early because my mom thought I was advanced."

A pause. It was rare of me to mention my mother. Finally she asked, "Were you?"

"Probably, but I'm not anymore."

She smiled, "So how are your grades these days, Charlie?"

She had never before asked me anything about school. It was such a normal thing to ask; it heartened me. It made me feel like maybe our relationship could be very simple—a teenager living with his nice grandmother. I felt even more hopeful about it. It was hard not to bring it up and ask her on the spot. I had already written the contract. But I knew it would be better to play it cool and save it for my next visit. Before I left, Mrs. M. said, "I hope you won't wait six years to come over again."

"I'll be back soon," I said. "Real soon."

♦ ♦ ♦

One week later, Mrs. M. sat beside me on her front porch, reading the contract. I was clutching the arms of the Adirondack chair, sweating bullets. She was surprised that I would ask her for something so huge—a place to live during my senior year. Her eyes were round as quarters behind her reading glasses, and she was scowling. But I remembered that a scowl from Mrs. M. didn't necessarily mean she would say no.

She finished reading, put the paper onto her lap, and looked away from me. There was a part of me that wanted to wrap my arms around her knees and beg her to take pity on me. But another part of me that knew this request had to be a business exchange—no drama—or it would never happen. "Tell me something, Charlie," she asked finally. "What will your dear father think about you moving in with me?"

"He won't care," I said. It was true; he had no use for me. He was completely distracted by a certain female teenager. And thirteen-year-old Liam hated me. I wouldn't miss either one of them. My mind was made up. If I could just live somewhere else, just start over, reinvent myself. If I could find a job, make a little money, finish high school, hide. If I could just not be connected in any way to any other Porters. Especially my dad, his insane mix of ambition, blindness, and meanness. I had a hunger for a few normal friends, maybe even a girlfriend who wasn't a fantasy. The chance to wake up anywhere, anywhere, but in that place, that bedroom I shared with Liam, that apartment, that drama queen Ruby, that sorry excuse for a father.

Mrs. M. interrupted my tortured thoughts. "You will not like living with me," she said, "especially under the conditions of your contract."

"Would you please just think about it, Mrs. M.?"

"You will be bored out of your mind here. And I am not fit company for most hours of most days."

"I already know that about you. But you're the only person on the whole planet that I could ask. Look, my dad is sleeping with a teenager, okay? It's making my home life really depraved. Really depraved, Mrs. M., worse than ever before."

This silenced her for a long minute. "Have you had any recent contact with your mother?" she asked.

"No, I have not."

"And you wouldn't consider asking her if she could help you with this situation?"

"I think you already know the answer to that question, Mrs. M."

"Charlie, moving in with me is a bad idea."

"Well, it's my only idea. You're my only hope. I swear to God I won't be any trouble."

"Well, I'm certainly not going to swear that *I* won't be any trouble! You won't like living with an old lady. It will drive you crazy."

"I'm already crazy, Mrs. M. I just really, really, really need a different place to live if I'm going to make it through my senior year without completely losing my mind. Nine short months, that's all I'm asking."

She pursed her lips, weakening.

Just say yes, I pleaded silently.

She said. "I have a condition."

I nodded, hope surging through my chest.

"If I am to be your new grandmother, then I require that you contact your mother and tell her what is happening to my other grandchild before you move in with me."

"*What?* She doesn't care about him! Nothing has changed."

"You may be right. But if you are going to leave your brother alone with your father and this . . . teenager, I at least want your mother to know about it."

"A big waste of time, Mrs. M."

"Take it or leave it."

I took it. "When can I move in?"

"When I have proof that you've contacted your mother."

She wasn't kidding. On the next Saturday, when I arrived with a trash bag full of belongings and a backpack stuffed with school supplies, she ordered me to write to my mother about Liam before I could take my things downstairs.

Grumbling, I sat down at her kitchen table and wrote this:

Mom [it killed me to call her "Mom," but what was I supposed to call her?],

I am moving out because I can't stand living with Dad. Liam will be stuck with him, and that will not be a good thing. You probably don't care. I will be living with a friend.

—Charlie

I handed it to Mrs. M. without looking at her.

"You need to add something about your father having a teenage girlfriend," she said.

"No, I don't."

"Yes, you do."

"Oh, crap. All right. Give it back to me." I took the note back and added, "P.S. Dad lives with a new girlfriend, who is still a teenager."

"Much better," she said.

She had tracked down an address for a Lucinda Jean Porter in Appleton, Wisconsin, the town I knew that Mom had moved to ten years ago. It had to be her. "Shall we put my return address on the envelope?" Mrs. M. asked.

"Hell, no!"

She frowned down at me in disapproval, and I glared back. Then she put the letter into an envelope with an exaggerated sigh. When I held out my hand for it, she said, "I will mail it, thank you very much. You may go downstairs and unpack now."

I went down into the basement, to my new room. The cement walls were painted white, the carpeting was new—indoor-outdoor grayish purple. There was one small egress window with a screen. A dresser, made of particle board, stood in one corner—the drawers worked. I began to fill it. A cot had been newly placed along one wall. Mrs. M. had bought me a new pillow—it was still in plastic on the mattress beside a small stack of sheets and three folded blankets. A small fan was still in the box on the floor.

Clean sheets, decent blankets, a new pillow, and a fan.

I don't know why exactly, but all of a sudden, I just lost it. I sat on the cot and cried with relief for what seemed like a whole hour. Then I couldn't go upstairs right away, so I was looking for something to distract me, and I noticed that there was a utility closet in one corner of the little room with a wooden door. My own closet. There was a bar across the top of the closet with several hangers. On the cement floor, toward the back wall, were two stacked boxes. I pulled back the flap of the one on top. It was full of *Franklin Firefly* books. I put the rest of my things on top of this box and put a couple of shirts on hangers. Hangers! Then I made up the bed. Then I went upstairs to have lunch in the kitchen with my new grandmother.

◆ ◆ ◆

"It was so busy at work! I'm exhausted. Let's get takeout tonight, okay? Hey! Are you even listening to me?"

"Sorry, sorry, I was . . . I've been . . . I thought a lot about Mrs. M. today."

"Me too! Didn't you say that she was an author? We should Google her! Does she have a website?"

"She wouldn't have a website. She hated that kind of stuff, and she quit writing completely about six years ago. She wrote this one book when she was younger. I can never remember the title—something with the words *night writer*. It was based on her dad being a reporter for the *Detroit Free Press* back in the sixties."

"Not *Every Night Writer*? Oh my God, Charlie, I read that book! We read it in my AP English class when I was in high school. Oh my God, I never made the connection! M. M. Manning, of course it's her!"

"Did you like the book?"

"I *loved* it. The girl's dad was a reporter during the Detroit riots and he almost gets killed trying to help some people and the little girl ends up writing about it and learning what it means to write from the heart. The ending is sad, though."

"Sad, how?"

"The father dies. The last chapter made me cry. God, how could somebody write something that good and then just decide not to write anymore?"

"She wrote some books after that. But she told me they didn't mean anything to her. She said she had realized that she was one of those writers with only one good book in them— one pure book, as she put it, but before she figured that out, she got on the author bandwagon and couldn't get off. So she wrote about bugs. Same thing I was doing. She said it would have been better for everyone, including her, if she had only written one book."

"You know what other book was like that? *To Kill a Mockingbird*. It was the only book Harper Lee ever wrote. Also *Wuthering Heights*. Two of my all-time favorite books."

"Did you ever read *Confederacy of Dunces*? That was a one-time book too. The author committed suicide because he was so depressed about not getting his novel published. I'm telling you, Clara, the book world is a dangerous place."

"Oh my God, Charlie, I just remembered something! At the end of *Every Night Writer*, the father gives the daughter his desk right before he dies!"

This silences me for a few beats. "Really?"

"Charlie, maybe Martha Manning gave you the same desk that her father gave to her! Like she totally believed you would become a famous writer! Probably because you were an author already!"

"No, I wasn't," I say quietly. "Not even close."

"Here we go again. When somebody writes a book, Charlie, then they are an author!"

"Clara . . . for God's sake—anybody can write anything and say it's a book!"

We are arguing, and I stop myself. I remember that Clara doesn't know the story behind the books. How much suffering they caused me. The real story. I haven't taken her back this far in time.

She isn't listening anymore; she's distracted and tired and hungry, pulling on her lip, frowning. I suspect that she is trying to figure out how we will get that huge and very important desk out of Mrs. M.'s house and where in the world it would fit in her house. Nowhere. I don't want it. I'm not a writer. I use a laptop, and I travel light. What on earth would I do with a desk like that?

NINETEEN

I notice a black trash bag under the table in one corner of Clara's kitchen. The trash bag moves slightly, and I realize it is a gigantic beetle curled up and trying to hide from me by looking like a trash bag. Its legs are curled up tight around its body. I am not afraid. I am annoyed. In the dream, I cry, "Hey! You! Quit hiding, I can see you!"

"Charlie, who are you talking to now?"

I pretend to still be asleep, sensing that Clara is now sitting up beside me in her bed. She gives my shoulder a gentle shake.

"Who's hiding, Charlie?"

I fake a soft snore. After a moment, Clara gives up and snuggles back in beside me. I am sleeping in her bed regularly now that my cast is off. It is the most wonderful thing, feeling her small perfect legs against my big hairy legs. My right ankle is still slightly sore, and she is always careful not to bump it. *Maybe this is going to work,* I think as I drift off. *Maybe this will keep going even after my injury is healed.*

◆◆◆

Clara comes home from work that same day and tells me something that causes a meltdown. We are facing each other in the kitchen, and I am furious. She is struggling to stay calm and reasonable, she doesn't understand my anger, and she doesn't like it. I am not mad at her—I am mad at Liam. I am squeezing my head in anger and muttering abuse. He has been calling my girlfriend "just to chat." He has called her three times on her cell phone since the time he broke into her house, which I haven't ever told her about. Clara says she has been meaning to mention his calls, but she was nervous that it might upset me. Good call, Clara! Jesus!

So today he calls her at work and INVITES her to his next big violin concert in Grand Rapids!

"I know. I know. I knew you'd be upset. But honestly, Charlie, I don't think there's anything wrong with him calling me—he was just being friendly."

"Aw, get a CLUE, Clara! And wait a minute, how does he even know you work at Rite Aid?"

"Would you stop yelling at me! Just stop it!"

"How does he know?"

"I guess I might have mentioned it when I was telling your mom where we met. I suppose he remembered."

"You should have hung up on him the first time he called you! You should have at LEAST told him never to call you again! Don't you see what he's trying to do? God, you're too nice, Clara! You're just too damn NICE!"

"I said, don't yell at me, Charlie Porter! Maybe I didn't WANT to hang up on him. He was just being friendly, and for your information, he wasn't just inviting ME to the concert, he was inviting both of us. And he said the whole thing was your mom's idea."

"That is such a fucking LIE!"

"Would you stop swearing? Why is it a lie? It could very well have been your mom's idea. Your mom seemed so . . . I mean, it was obviously important to her that we all got together that one time."

"Mom wouldn't have invited us. She would have left it up to us when we wanted to see her again. She'd take it slow. She's just really . . . shy."

Shy. The small word hung in the air between us, and for a brief moment, I saw Mom's face, her young face—pale, uncertain, shy. I was her helpful son, staying close to her skirts but helping her in the outside world, holding her hand, helping her with her new baby, finding her inhaler. What had Dad done to her to make her do something so irreversibly unmotherly as to leave her children behind? I knew what Dad had done to me and to Liam. What had he done to Mom?

Clara is watching me. She says softly, "You're shy too, Charlie. You were really shy when we first met. I loved that about you."

I don't respond. I feel suddenly miserably sad. Too sad to move. Too sad to speak. Is it because I had an extended, sympathetic thought about my mother, something I have for so long made a point never to do? Now I'm thinking about her, seeing her. She is wearing a soft, tweedy sweater with leather buttons that I still remember. She called it her Mary Poppins sweater. *Mary Poppins* was her favorite movie. She is putting on the sweater, buttoning it up, and preparing to fly.

Clara touches my arm.

"Hey, you. Don't look so sad. Look, if your brother calls me again, I'll tell him I'm too busy to talk, okay?"

"Please don't talk to him anymore."

"I guess this means we won't be going to his concert."

"No, we are not going to his concert."

I put my elbows on the table and lower my head into my arms. "I feel like too much is happening to me, Clara. Too many past disasters hanging over my head. Next thing you know, my dad will probably call us and say he's back in the States and ask if he can live here with us. Seriously!"

Incredibly, at that exact moment, the phone rings. Clara's eyes grow round in alarm. She gasps, "He can't live here, Charlie!"

Then we start to laugh. Nervous laughter, because we don't recognize the number on Clara's caller ID.

"Oh my God, Charlie. Should I answer it?"

But she waits too long, and it goes into voice mail and we listen to the message and it is the Grandville Surgical Clinic, calling to tell Clara that in regards to a Mrs. Martha Manning in Cedar Rapids, Iowa, the clinic is not able to give out phone numbers to nonpatients.

Clara looks guilty as charged. "I just thought . . . I just thought we should . . . I just wanted to . . ."

"Jesus, Clara. Why didn't you just ask me for her number?"

"Oh, you have it? Could you go get it?"

I glare at her.

"Don't look at me like that, Charlie, I wasn't going to call her without telling you!"

"No, no, go ahead and call her," I say. "I'll get the number for you. Seriously, call her right now."

"Charlie . . . don't be like this. I just thought we should thank her."

"Oh sure, thank her! Ask her if she wants to go with you to Liam's concert. She loves violin music." And this is true. She played violin concertos in the mornings—Mozart and Schumann and Liszt, part of her morning routine, which became my morning routine for that blissful year. And all that time, all those mornings, my brother was ten miles away, living with our mother, playing the violin every day, and waiting to get his revenge.

Clara is asking me something. "Cheese and mushrooms? Charlie? Where are you, Charlie? Oh, be that way. I'm ordering cheese and mushrooms. And get me that number—now!"

She orders the pizza. While she is on the phone, I retrieve Mrs. M.'s phone number—written on an index card in one of the boxes. She gave it to me before she left Michigan. Clara is on hold. I flash the number in front of her face. She snaps the card out of my hand. Frowning. Then takes a pen from her cup of pens and writes in large letters above the number: "MARTHA MANNING'S PHONE #." The pen she is using just happens to be Mrs. M.'s diamond pen. Apparently, it still works.

◆◆◆

Mrs. M. was wrong to think I wouldn't like living with her. I liked it from day one. I liked her cozy house. I liked my room in the basement. I liked her simple cooking and her sandwiches. I liked watching TV with her in the evenings (she was obsessed with crime shows). I slept like a log on my little bed and appreciated not having to hear people having sex in the next room.

My bathroom was a tad dingy, but I was used to a much worse one, and in the basement, I had complete privacy, nobody ever pounding on the door for me to hurry up and no female products overflowing from a shared cabinet.

During the first month, Mrs. M. bought a few other things for my room without asking—a little computer desk, a small bookshelf, an old stuffed chair, an alarm clock, and a clip-on lamp that could attach to the top of the stuffed chair for night reading. Whenever she would buy something for me, she would tell me that she bought it with her latest huge royalty check because she was such a successful author. It was a game with us.

The chores I had contracted to do were normal and finishable, especially compared to the unfixable mess I had come from. Taking out her trash took five minutes. Raking her leaves was a piece of cake—she had a nice new rake and a wheelbarrow. Apparently, her husband had been kind of a garage neatnik, and she had the most well-stocked tool and yard shed that I could have ever imagined. Everything I did in that little house made sense and felt easy. My homework was easier. Sleeping was easier. I learned to cook a few simple things. I recycled. I learned how to use a food processor. Me!

Mrs. M.'s garage became a secret world of delights. Everything in it worked—nothing was broken. A shiny-new power mower, an assortment of clean buckets, and tools hanging from a shelf in symmetrical rows. I learned how to use many of them. I fixed things—a broken cupboard door, a leaky faucet, a section of loose floorboard on one end of her front porch. I got handier and faster and always put my tools back in the places where I had found them.

Mrs. M. always acted amazed that I would do any of these

things without being asked. She would say, "It's not even in the contract, Charlie."

"We don't have to be slaves to the contract, Mrs. M."

My senior year of school was strange but manageable. I was getting along better with my peers. A few of my teachers were openly nice to me. I got a few As, mostly in my English classes. Ironically, the librarian liked me. A couple of girls seemed interested in me and invited me to their parties. I went, although I mostly stayed hidden in dark corners. I wasn't a beetle anymore, but now I had another secret—that my father had stolen the last babysitter from me and kept her for himself. I had seen too much. I knew too much about sex, although until that year, I never had any. I was afraid that the truth of this showed on my face, especially when I was trying to be charming.

Slowly that year, I reinvented myself—a serious guy with a streak of dry humor who lived alone with his odd, lovable grandmother and kept his sordid past firmly in the past. I got better at just being a teenager in high school. I learned to make small talk and be ironic. I accepted the possibility that I was reasonably good-looking. I had a few random sexual experiences that weren't disastrous, just predictably meaningless. Nobody questioned my family situation; lots of kids at my high school lived with relatives.

Once, at a party—one of those parents-away-for-the-weekend-somebody-got-a-keg events—I noticed a girl trying to catch my eye as I wandered around the house, nursing a red cup of something vile. After half an hour, I finally let her corner me in the kitchen. A few minutes of the usual high school small talk, and then she swerved into unsafe territory.

"If you live with your gram, where is the rest of your

family?" Her eyes widened in alarm as she waited for my answer. No one had ever asked me so directly. I realized it was a moment of either truth or nontruth. I opted for exotic appeal: "They are no longer with me."

Her jaw dropped. "You mean . . ."

I looked deep into her eyes with all the sadness I could muster. Then slowly looked away, without answering. It worked.

She said, "Oh my God, Charlie."

I shrugged sorrowfully.

She put down her own red cup and picked up my hand and entwined our fingers meaningfully. She would comfort me, at least for a little while.

After that I started routinely telling my classmates and my teachers that Mrs. M. was my only living relative, and the more I said it, the more true it seemed. Soon only Mrs. M. knew that I had a brother—she still asked about Liam from time to time, and I told her that I was keeping in touch with him and that I would bring him over soon but then always had a plausible reason for why it wasn't a good time. I could no more have gone back to that apartment for Liam than I could have gone back to check in with Ruby. I did my best to forget them.

Then, in the spring of that same year, amazingly, I got a job. I had studied up on the tools needed to fix bicycles and learned the names of all the hottest cycle brands and I was friendly and relaxed during the job interview and it worked! The bike shop was next to the Rite Aid, and I started working twenty hours a week, after school and Saturdays. I started right away giving Mrs. M. a token amount of money from my paycheck, and she took it and said that she was proud of me for getting a job "without having any helpful connections."

I was still working at the bike shop during the fall after I had moved into the motel, and I started to go to the Rite Aid rather frequently, even when I didn't need anything, because a certain pharmacist's assistant always smiled and said hello to me. I was completely smitten with her in her white lab coat with her tortoiseshell glasses and her thick auburn hair, always worn in a big twist halfway up the back of her head. Fantastic hair. I used to wish there was something wrong with me so I could order a prescription from her. Antibiotics! Fungus cream! Sodium pentothal!

Finally, one afternoon I got up the nerve to ask her where the Band-Aids were, and then I followed her, watching her walk from a few steps behind her in a state of shock and awe. She stopped at the bandages section of the aisle and turned around and smiled for a longer beat than usual, like it was so enjoyable to help me. She wore a name tag on the lapel of her lab coat that said *Clara*.

She noticed that I was staring at it. "Where's *your* name tag?" she asked.

"We don't wear them at the bike shop," I said. "But my name is actually Charlie."

"You work at Bodacious Bikes? No wonder I see you all the time."

"It's very dangerous work. I'm always needing Band-Aids."

She laughed. It completely astounded me. It gave me the courage of a tiger. "Would you ever want to have lunch with me?" I asked her, and I said her name for the first time: *Clara*.

TWENTY

I am grocery shopping at the neighborhood store for the first time in the two months I have lived with Clara, pushing a cart and checking off a list of groceries. I have decided that it's time for me to start cooking dinner for Clara, now that I can get around on my own. I'd learned to cook a few things, living with Mrs. M., although I am rusty and Mrs. M. had a much better kitchen. But I am determined to start doing my share.

Halfway through the list, I hear someone call my name, and this surprises me. Nobody knows me by name in Clara's neighborhood.

"Charlie Porter!" someone calls. "Is that you, Charlie? It's me, Sam Church!"

Someone is coming toward me—someone too old to be Sam Church, but it is Sam Church, my once illustrator. One of the few people in this town who might recognize me in a grocery store. I happen to know that my dad never paid him for his final contribution to my career. As he comes closer, he glances down at my walking boot and asks, "What the hell did you do to your foot, Charlie?"

"Achilles tendon," I say. Otherwise, I would run from him. He has outstretched his hand to shake mine, no escape. I shake it.

"Sorry to hear that," he says. He adds meaningfully, "Remember me?"

"You're Sam," I say. "My dad's friend."

Sam is not aging well. He has let his hair grow way too long—like crazy, never-wash-it-or-comb-it long, and he is wearing a battered khaki hat tied under his double chin and his face is that kind of red-purple that people's faces get when they drink all the time. No surprise. He was one of my dad's few drinking buddies, after all. Maybe the only one.

"So what d'ya hear these days from the old man?" he asks.

"I think he lives in Jamaica," I reply.

"I *know* he lives in Jamaica," says Sam. And so at last I know that my dad does indeed live in Jamaica. Instantly, I wish I didn't know; I preferred not being sure.

"Yeah, we stayed in touch for a little while," Sam continues. "He was always gonna send me that money. You know. For doin' the illustrations."

"I don't know anything about that," I say.

"Somebody told me that old Dan got your little brother to do the same gig as you. That youngest-published-author gig. So there must still be books around, right? Money comin' in, right?"

"I don't think so," I say. "I moved out a long time ago, and I didn't stay in touch with them. I don't even know my dad's address."

"You probably know he married that little girl once he got down to Jamaica, right? What was her name?"

"I don't know," I say.

"Your dad owes me like over two thousand dollars, Charlie. For the work I did on those last two books. Do you think you could find out how I can get ahold of him?"

"I don't know where he is," I say. "I'm sorry he didn't pay you. He was really, really bad with money."

Sam Church's expression darkens. He says, "I was supposed to get half. I sure as hell didn't get half."

"I didn't get anything," I say, equally bitter. "Except a really fucked-up childhood."

Sam takes a step away from me, shocked. I take this moment to depart, needing to be finished with him, and he calls after me, finding his voice. "Well, if you ever do talk to your dad, tell him to call me. I'm still at the same copy shop. He can call me there."

◆ ◆ ◆

When I get back to the apartment, I am terribly anxious. It is that feeling again—too many things coming together at once. Clara has left the index card with Mrs. M.'s phone number taped to the kitchen counter. Does she expect me to call Mrs. M.? Just pick up the phone and call her? Does she have any idea how hard it would be for me to do that? Mrs. M. might not want to talk to me. Or her sister might answer and tell me she just died like an hour ago. There is absolutely no way that I can dial her number. I pull the card off the counter and hide it in a drawer.

◆ ◆ ◆

Clara's parents have picked the night and restaurant for our gathering; I'm sure they can't wait to grill me about when I am planning to stop being a deadbeat. Clara keeps insisting that they like me.

"No really, they want to celebrate that you're doing so much better. Come on! It'll be fun!"

She writes the occasion down on the small Michigan Wonderland calendar she keeps on the fridge: "6:30 dinner with Mom and Dad at Casey's Bistro." One week from today. With a smiley face. She is using Mrs. M.'s pen again. My life is insane.

◆ ◆ ◆

I am waking up from a nap when I hear someone walking around in the kitchen. At first, I think I'm in a beetle dream, but then I realize I'm not dreaming; I'm hearing the sounds of someone in the kitchen who is not Clara, someone making no effort to be silent. I hear cups and saucers clattering. After a moment, I hear the whistle of the teakettle. I groan into my pillow.

I lurch to the kitchen without my boot. The kitchen window is open again. The screen is on the floor again. Liam is pouring water into the teakettle. "Hey, Big Brother!" His smile is ear to ear. I hate that smile, that slick Porter smile. "Rise and shine! Don't you ever get tired of sleeping all day?"

"I don't sleep all day," I say. "And you broke into Clara's house again. This is not cool, Liam."

"I'm just making tea," he says. "Black tea. A little caffeine to help you wake up. You need to get some better tea, bro. Mom only uses loose tea; she's kind of a fanatic. Your hot girlfriend scored major points with her, making her tea."

"Don't talk about Clara. And stop calling her at work. It's really bothering her. She doesn't like it."

"Oh, no, she likes it. We've had some really nice conversations. She's very curious about me, very impressed."

"No, she isn't, Liam."

"Actually, she is! I invited her to my next concert—at Aquinas College—a very big deal—but then she never called me back so, I thought, why not just head over there and talk it over with Charlie. Over a nice cup of tea. I really think you need to come, bro. I think you might be sorry if you don't." He is smiling, but it is clearly a threat.

"Jesus, Liam. What is wrong with you? You can't just sneak inside Clara's house like this and you can't call her and you can't threaten me into going to one of your goddamn CONCERTS!"

Suddenly we are both yelling.

"Oh, are you THREATENED? Am I THREATENING you? Are you SCARED?"

"GET OUT OF HERE! Go back out through the window like the CRIMINAL you are!"

We stand head-to-head, facing each other. It feels like a very bad dream. I am waiting for a beetle to come clicking and clacking around the corner. Liam is breathing heavily. He is clenching and unclenching his fist. He looks like what he wants to do most in the world is punch me. What I want is to push him headfirst back out the window. But a part of me, maybe the more adult part of me, realizes that we both have to calm down. We can't fight. We can't be screaming at each other. It's too dangerous.

I hold up my hands, a truce gesture. And I say, more calmly, "Look, I'm sorry. I'm sorry I lost my temper. But you're trying to freak me out on purpose, breaking in like this when Clara's not here and calling her and inviting her to concerts and it's working, Liam. It's freaking me out, and I want you to stop it."

Liam's eyes narrow. He says, "You don't deserve her."

"I know I don't deserve her. I am the first person to admit it. But you can't be playing games with her to get back at me."

"Get back at you?" he sneers. "Why would I need to get back at you?"

I admit, with a huge effort, "For all the shit I did to you . . . back then."

I think it catches him off guard. Almost an apology. Almost. He lets it sink in. Then he asks calmly, "You mean before you left? Or after you left?"

"I mean . . . I mean . . . all of it. All of it, Liam. Please, I know you hate me, but you have to quit playing these games with Clara."

"I'm not playing games, Charlie. I don't have time for games. I'm leaving in a month for Interlochen. You won't be seeing me for a while once I move up there. So relax! Drink some tea with me. Sit down. How's the leg?"

Warily, I sit down. He slowly and carefully pours me a cup of black tea.

"Mom has this really old blue teapot. I guess it was her gram's. Do you remember it?"

He looks up at me as he pours his own cup, gauging how I will take this mention of Mom. I say, quietly, "I remember it."

"She sure drinks a lot of tea. She is going to be drinking it completely by herself after I leave. I've been telling her she should look for a roommate. Or join a church again or something."

"She quit going to church?"

"Oh yeah. Long time ago. Still prays all the time, though. Mostly for you."

"Jesus. Don't tell me that."

"You should come over and see her. Come after I'm gone. I know you like to pretend I don't exist."

"I told you how I feel about this already, Liam."

He takes a final slurp of tea and walks away from the table. The photo of Rita, still on the fridge door catches his eye. He looks at it for a moment, then snatches it off the fridge, tears it into two pieces, and throws it in the trash on his way to the front door.

◆ ◆ ◆

I am in the Green Grove apartment at the doorway to my bedroom. Liam is already asleep, under the covers on his side of our bedroom, surrounded by knives and guns. I realize from this that he knows about the giant beetle living in our house. He has figured it out without me telling him. I am glad he knows, and I am not the only one afraid. I think that I will borrow a few weapons from his bed to keep on my side of the room. But as I approach him, I hear a loud, raspy breathing sound coming from under his bed. One gigantic leg is sticking out, the claw on the end of it, flexing and unflexing, like a metal hook. I am thinking, I can crush its leg with my walking boot and then it will be crippled. I can do that. I can do that for Liam.

But I can't move and I can't move and the whirring gets louder and I stand frozen in my old bedroom and it is my own raspy, tortured breathing that finally wakes me up.

TWENTY-ONE

I was right—it is not as intense to be with Clara's parents in a restaurant. We are seated at a four-top in a quiet corner of Casey's, a local family eatery, and it turns out that our waitress Marie is an old high school friend of Clara's and so there is an initial exchange of happiness and amazement and I am introduced to Marie by Clara as her boyfriend, a word that never fails to astound me.

Don tells Marie to put the tab on one check and then aside, he says to me, "You're probably going to want a big old steak, eh Charlie?"

"Charlie's a vegetarian," Clara says brightly. "I told you that before, Dad."

Don gives me a fleeting look of bewilderment. Then he smiles coldly. After we put our dinner order in, he turns back to me with renewed determination to find out what the hell is wrong with me. "So, Charlie," he begins. "You seem to be getting around pretty well with that boot thing. When will you be headed back to the office?"

"He works at a bike shop, remember? Bodacious Bikes near where I work."

"My apologies, you did tell me that, but it slipped my mind." Back to me, "So when do you see yourself starting back to work at this bike shop?"

"Soon as the boot comes off, Mr. Morrison. It really limits my mobility, and we do so much kneeling and squatting and lifting, you know, working on the bicycles."

"That makes sense, Don," says Sue.

"He's a little better every day. Aren't you, Charlie?"

"I sure am." And right after I say this, right after I agree without any irony or deceit that I'm doing better every day, I hear a familiar voice call my name and I look up from the group and I see Liam coming toward us in the restaurant and I realize in a flash that a few steps behind him, looking extremely uncomfortable and trapped, is my mother, Lucinda. Liam and Mom. Mom and Liam.

My mom hangs back, but Liam walks up to our table, stands behind Clara, puts a hand on one of her shoulders and gives it a squeeze. Like they are best buds. Clara meets my eyes. I recognize her fear from the first meeting with Mom and Liam, and I can see it growing.

"I'm not late, am I?" Liam asks, clapping his hands together, and again, I feel as though I am caught in a dream; will a long black leg poke me from under our table?

A round of Morrison sputtering ensues. Clara finally begins speaking in sentences. "We weren't expecting you, Liam. But since you're here—okay—Mom, Dad, this is Charlie's brother, Liam."

"Really nice to meet you." He stretches his long arm across the table to shake hands with Don and Sue. Then he turns to Mom, who is still hanging back a few tables away. She looks as though she is about to pass out from shyness. She is wearing an ancient shirt—a shirt I remember from before she left—buttoned up to her chin and one of those triangle kerchiefs covering her hair, like she's Amish. She looks like she's wearing a costume. I recognize every symptom of her terror at finding herself in the middle of a grotesque show—the centerpiece of someone else's scheme. Another trap. And she is blaming herself; somehow I know this. Liam actually steps away from the table, takes her hand, and pulls her toward us.

"And this is our mom, Lucinda Porter," he says. He looks directly at me. Our mother is his weapon.

"Hi, Mrs. Porter. These are my parents, Sue and Don Morrison."

"What are you folks doing here in Hudsonville?" Sue asks, obviously confused. "Are you visiting?"

"We just live over in Grand Rapids," Liam says. "Not far at all."

Lucinda takes a step away from the table, away from us. She has realized the situation's impossibility, and she is making her move, reaching beyond her shyness to make a clean getaway. She says, with what I can see is a superhuman effort, "Very nice to meet you all, hope you have a nice dinner." Then she turns on her heel and retraces her steps through the maze of restaurant tables, exiting without once looking back at Liam.

Liam looks aggravated. Thwarted. There is an incredibly long, awkward moment during which I am looking at my lap, feeling blood pulsing angrily through my neck and face. There is not one safe person for me to look at right now in the entire universe. I am bracing myself to look at Clara, but part of me is afraid to lift my head, because if Liam's hand is still on her shoulder, I believe I will fly across the table and break his nose.

Again, it is Clara who breaks the silence. "Maybe, you'd better go after your mom, Liam. She can't exactly go anywhere without you."

My head is still lowered. I clench my jaw, wondering how Clara knows that my mother doesn't drive when I didn't tell her that my mother doesn't drive.

"Right you are," Liam says. "Gotta run. Nice to meet you, Mr. and Mrs. Morrison. Have a great dinner. Some other time, Clara, thanks for the invite. Good to see you, brother. Take care of that leg!"

And he is gone. I take a deep breath and raise my head and look at Clara. She is looking off to the side, staring away from our table, observing another family. Her mother is patting her hand in confusion. Clara will not meet my eyes. Her dad begins to drum his fingers on the table, preparing to speak.

"You know," he begins, "I was under the impression that . . .

Just then, Marie comes back to the table. "Was someone going to join you?" she asks cheerfully.

"Absolutely not," I insist.

"Well, then, are you folks ready to order?"

The Morrisons order. I order last. I ask for the chicken pasta without the chicken and hand Marie my menu, giving her a big fake Porter smile. Sue and Don are watching me, waiting for an explanation for what just happened. I say, "I have no idea why they were here, and I don't know why my estranged brother was being so . . . overly friendly."

"Estranged?" Sue echoes. "Are you estranged from your brother, dear?"

"Yes, I am. He is not to be trusted." I am looking at Clara as I say this.

"Well, *that's* too bad," Sue decides.

"I thought you said you don't have other relatives living around here," Don grumbles.

"I don't," I say. "They live way on the other side of Grand Rapids, and I try to avoid them. My brother tricked my mom into coming with him to this restaurant today for some reason that I do not know. Do you know, Clara?"

Clara looks at me, finally. Her eyes are sad, but not sad for me. She looks suddenly ten years older, a disappointed woman. A woman who is giving up on something.

◆ ◆ ◆

Back at Clara's house, I am sitting on a stoop at the back door, unwilling to go inside, unwilling to talk, unwilling to leave, trapped with my anger at Liam—and at Clara—trapped with the knowledge that I will be needing another place to live soon, a huge complication since I have no job and no money.

I sit alone with my head in my arms until Clara comes out and sits beside me on the step. She has been crying a long time, but her voice is firm.

"We have to talk, Charlie. I know what you're thinking, and you're wrong. I did *not* invite your brother to Casey's tonight. I would *never* have invited him without asking you. I was just as surprised as you were when he walked in."

I don't believe her. I can't even look at her. Liam got to her. Liam found out from her about our dinner. There was no other way for him to know. I lift my head and ask, "Did you ever like . . . meet up with him? Since that time they were here? Like just the two of you somewhere?"

"Why would I do that, Charlie? You asked me not to, remember?"

"Did he ever ask you to meet him somewhere? Alone?"

"Well . . . he did that once, when he first called me, but I made up an excuse. I knew you wouldn't like that."

My mind darkens. He tried to meet with her alone.

"Charlie, he's fifteen. He's really immature. He doesn't know the rules. He just wants to get closer to us, like any normal brother would."

Like any normal brother. Suddenly, it's like Clara is wearing a sign on her forehead that says *NORMAL PERSON*. It is why she is so completely trusting and gullible. It's why she wants to include Liam in our relationship. It is why she got mixed up with someone like me in the first place.

I want her to see once and for all that she is not dealing with normal people. There is nothing normal about the Porter family. So I look her squarely in her red-rimmed eyes, and I say, "Here's a little something you don't know about my family, Clara. The last babysitter we had—Ruby—she wasn't really a babysitter. Dad called her our babysitter, but really she was this crazy messed-up teenager that my dad got interested in. Interested as in having sex with her. Like, constantly. Because having sex with a goddamn kid made him feel young again. It was one of the reasons I begged Mrs. M. to let me live with her. I left Liam behind, and I never once went back to the apartment. I never saw him. I never called him. I never checked on him. And he hates me for that, Clara.

He hates me for that, and I don't blame him, but now he's trying to get back at me. That's why he's been calling you. He wants to hurt me like I hurt him. That's why he brought Mom to Casey's. That's why you should never have told him we would be there."

There is a long and dreadful silence. I add, bitterly, "So sorry your little experiment was a flop."

Clara stands up.

"You think I would do something like that just for an experiment? You think I would lie to you? Charlie, *you're* the one who has lied and lied and told crazy stories and left out important facts—and now you're calling me a liar? You know what? You know what? I don't think I can do this anymore. I don't think I can be your girlfriend. I can't stand finding out all this horrible stuff about you in these horrible ways, where I ask and I ask and I ask and finally it comes out of the blue and hits me in the face and it's always bad. It's always really bad, Charlie. Your dad was sleeping with the *babysitter*? No, I really, really can't take it anymore."

"Look, I come from a different universe than you," I admit. "And mine keeps sucking me back down into the dirt. My brother, my mom, my dad, all these memories and stupid dreams about beetles, everything piling up . . ."

"Wait, *what*? You have dreams about beetles? Like the beetles you wrote books about?"

"Not cartoon beetles, Clara. I'm talking about giant insects trying to find me and kill me. I had one last night. I was back in the old apartment where I lived with Dad and Liam and there was a huge beetle hiding under Liam's bed and I couldn't do anything about it and—"

She covers her ears. "Stop!" she cries. "You said your nightmares were from the meds, Charlie. You said it a million times! Why are you still having nightmares? Why couldn't you tell me before now? It's too late, Charlie. It's too late. It's over. Do you hear me? It's over. I don't want to know anything else about you."

She goes back into the house. I hear a noise then, coming from inside. It has an ancient, eerie familiarity, the faint, watery vibrato sounds of someone sobbing uncontrollably from a distant room.

TWENTY-TWO

The next few days are filled with icy silences and general misery. I sleep on the sofa. Clara leaves for work without saying good-bye. She doesn't ask me if I'm hungry. She's basically not speaking to me at all, but at one point, while I am looking through local job notices on my laptop, she comes into the kitchen and asks me where the photo of that girl is. The one that used to be on the fridge. A crushing question, since I had never mentioned to her that Liam has twice broken into her house. It seems a terrible idea to tell her about it now, with the subject of Liam like a ticking bomb between us.

So instead, I make a show of getting up from the kitchen table, looking at the fridge door with a puzzled expression—where could Rita have gone? And while I am performing this charade, I notice that the Michigan Wonderland calendar is right beside the empty space where the photo of Rita used to be. And right on this calendar—in plain view of all intruders and terrorists—it is written that Charlie and Clara will be having dinner with the parents at Casey's Bistro on a Tuesday night at 6:30 p.m.

A terrible regret washes over me. I was wrong, I was wrong, I was wrong. Clara would never lie. But she's right. It's too late. Too late to take back my accusations. Why was I so sure that Liam had gotten to Clara? Why didn't I believe her? Was it because I feel so much like I deserve Liam's treachery? I turn to look at her, she looks deadly serious, and my hopelessness must be showing on my unshaven face.

"Oh, don't give me that pathetic look, Charlie. Just tell me where you put that photo. Did you put it back in your precious box?"

I simply cannot find the words to answer her. I feel like there is a mountain of ash between me and all the things I still need to tell her and I will never get around it, never. She shrugs, unsurprised by my reticence, and leaves the room again. After a moment, the landline rings, and it is her mom. Clara takes the call into another room. Muffled tones. Her mom is calling every day, asking her how "the Project" is going, "the Project" being getting Charlie the hell out of her house, now that Clara's time of slavery to my needs is over, thank goodness for everyone involved. The Morrisons are anxious to help. They are ready and willing with the truck. Not that a truck is in any way necessary. I have almost nothing to pack. The only piece of furniture I own is a desk that exists in another location, from another lifetime.

What would I do with a desk like that?

◆ ◆ ◆

On day three of the Project, I drag myself off the sleeper sofa after Clara has left for work, and I see through the living room picture window that there are two large boxes on the front porch. At the front door I notice that a note is taped to the top box, folded in half. I pull it off and I unfold it, knowing in advance that it will upset me. The note, if you can believe this, is from a scratch pad with a Sam Church image of Beetle Boy sitting back on his wing parts, squinting through his glasses, reading a book. Dad must have made personal stationery for Liam/Charlie. Under the cartoon beetle, a line of text reads: from the desk of Charlie Porter, World's Youngest Published Author.

And under this is Liam's message: "I'll bet your girlfriend is dying to read these. You should warn her, though, they suck."

Mother of God. The last thing in the world I want to deal with right now. But an idea comes to me—I go back inside, look up an address in Grand Rapids and get dressed and call a cab—expensive, but I have no choice. When the cabbie comes, I am waiting for him in front of Clara's house, two boxes on the curb.

◆ ◆ ◆

"Hey, I been thinkin' about you since I bumped into you last week," Sam Church says from behind the counter at Printing Express. "I felt kinda bad with what you said to me about your childhood."

Sam and I take the boxes and carry them to the back of the shop. I've been inside the copy store for ten minutes, and the fumes are already getting to me. No wonder Sam looks old before his time. Today he is wearing a baseball hat with a scraggly gray ponytail pulled through the loop at the back. The whites of his eyes are way too yellow.

"Your dad was my friend, Charlie. We had some good times. I always figured you boys were okay, having such a fun-lovin' dad. And I guess I just assumed you were as much into the whole bug book thing as he was."

"Sorry, but I hated it. It was horrible for me. I was such an introverted kid. Plus, I was in shock that my mom had left me. Those stories were her bedtime stories, and I always felt like I was stealing them."

His jaw drops. "Wow, I did not know any of that. You kids seemed to be doing fine without her."

"We weren't fine. Nope. Not even close."

"Well, do you ever see your mom now? What was her name again?"

"Lucinda. Actually she lives with my little brother somewhere in Grand Rapids."

"Man, I could never figure out how your parents *ever* got together. Dan was such a wild guy. He could party all night. And she was—what did you call it? Introverted? She was real introverted too. And very nervous. A nervous woman. Everything bothered her. I wasn't surprised when she split on him. I was just surprised that she didn't take you kids with her. That's what the women usually do."

"Right," I agreed. "Very puzzling."

"Well . . . I don't really know what I'm gonna do with all these books, but I'll think of something."

"You should sell them on eBay, Sam. Lots of people sell books on eBay. I had a friend once who sold her books in batches of ten at a reduced price—she sold all of them pretty fast."

"Do you know how to do that?" he asked hopefully.

"No clue," I lied. "But ask around. It's easy to find people who will know how to help you get them listed."

"Hmmm. I just might give it a try. I really appreciate you giving them to me, Charlie, when you could have just sold them yourself." He was shaking my hand as he said this; we were even-steven.

◆ ◆ ◆

It had been my brilliant idea to sell the *Franklin Firefly* books in my closet on eBay. I had read an article on the Internet about making money off books this way, especially if they were new. Apparently, teachers and librarians often trolled auction sites looking for multiple copies of books to use in reading groups. I explained all of this to Mrs. M. "The article suggested batches of ten, shipped book rate in cheap padded mailers," I said.

"I prefer not to be involved in this project," Mrs. M. insisted. "Honestly, just seeing those ridiculous books makes me ill. Plus, they remind me of a terrible time in my life."

"You mean when you met me? That was such a terrible time?"

"Meeting you wasn't terrible," she said. "Annoying, yes, but ultimately rewarding. But everything else that year was pretty bad."

"You mean because of your husband dying?"

"No, no, that had happened long before. No, I had a very serious illness the year before I met you. I was recovering when we met. Trying to get my life back on track. Unfortunately, I chose the wrong way." She shuddered and added, "The *Franklin Firefly* way."

As she was speaking, something was coming into my head, an earlier image of her, the way she had looked when I'd met her. Her paleness and thinness and her constant scowling and that terrible red wig. I was older now, old enough to know what it meant when a woman is very pale and thin and has no hair.

I asked softly, "Did you have cancer before I met you, Mrs. M.?"

"I did."

"Geez. Why didn't you ever mention it before today?"

"I don't know. I hadn't planned on mentioning it today. It's not something I need to talk about. And I certainly wasn't about to dump it on you when I first met you, for God's sake. You had enough to worry about, poor little orphan in a bug suit that you were."

"So you had that chemotherapy thing? Where your hair falls out?"

"Lots of chemotherapy, Charlie. A tough year."

We needed suddenly to look away from each other. But I managed to say, "Mrs. M., if I had known you that year, I would have helped you."

"I think maybe I needed you more the year after. When we did meet. When I was in *Franklin Firefly* hell."

"And I was in *Beetle Boy* hell. And you kept calling my dad a pimp and insulting all the librarians and telling me to get away from you."

She smiled and patted my hand. "Such sweet memories you have of me."

◆ ◆ ◆

When I return home from the Printing Express, I do something that I have been slowly building up the courage to do over the past few weeks, even before my brother destroyed my relationship with my girlfriend, even before I became a man with no place to live. I lean against the counter in Clara's kitchen and punch a phone number into the landline, noticing that my phone hand is shaking like I'm an old person. *Just one old person calling another old person*, I reassure myself and take a deep breath and wait through several rings.

A voice I don't recognize answers, and I ask for Martha. It feels very strange to say "Martha," but the person who answers says, "Just a minute."

A few minutes later: "Hello, this is Martha."

"You'll never guess who this is."

"Wrong. I know it's you. Took you long enough. How is your leg?"

"How did you even know about my accident, Mrs. M.?"

"Mr. Carter told me. I asked him to keep an eye on the house and gave him my sister's phone number. Apparently, he saw you flailing in the street in front of my house, and he thinks you're my grandson, so he called me. The hospital told me who your surgeon was. I knew you didn't have any health insurance, and I didn't want you drowning in debt. So is your leg getting better? No complications?"

"No complications, just a very impressive scar. Listen, I have a few things I need to say to you right away. Like, before we can converse normally. First of all, thank you for paying my medical bills. I know it's a ton of money to pay for an operation. But someday I'll pay you back, I swear I will."

"Not to worry, Charlie. I'll have plenty of money once the house is sold."

"The second thing I need to say right away is that once I read the letter you left for me, I thought you were dead. I really thought you were dead, Mrs. M. That's why I ran into the street and hurt my leg. And that's why you haven't heard from me. For a while I was too mad at you to write to you, but then I met this girl and got all caught up in that and then you basically told me in the note that you were dead!"

"I know. I know. Perhaps I overdid it. But I honestly didn't think I'd last more than a month or two after I moved. And we parted on such bad terms, Charlie. I wanted to correct that. I wanted to give you a memorable good-bye gift, something that would live on after my death."

"But, Mrs. M.! What if I had never gone back to the house because I was still too mad at you to go back there? I would never have even *seen* that note!"

"Oh, I knew you'd go back. You're a very morbid person, Charlie—I could totally picture you sneaking back into the house in the darkness."

"It *wasn't* dark! It was broad daylight! And it almost never happened! And you should have told me before you left that you were dying instead of telling me in a note!"

"If you recall, Charlie, we were having a hard time talking to each other about anything before I left."

"I didn't want you to go. I wanted you to let me help you. I would have taken care of you, Mrs. M."

"Charlie, you have no idea what you're saying. You have no idea how hard that would have been for us."

This silences me. I suppose she is right. "Well, I don't know why you're giving me your dad's desk."

She's quiet for a minute, then, "My dad's desk? Who said anything about it being my dad's? My husband bought it for me, and I secretly hated it. It's hideous but very valuable. English mahogany from the turn of the century. I figured you could sell it."

"Sell it! You mean, keep the money?"

"Keep the money, Charlie. Get out of the motel. Take some classes. Get some training. You have so much potential."

"But how do I sell an antique desk?"

"It's a project for you, Charlie. Move the desk to a safe storage unit and look into it. Ask my neighbor Frank if you need the names of some local antique dealers."

"You really wouldn't mind if I sold it?"

"I would be happy if you sold it."

"My next question is: do you think you might ever come back here?"

"I'm not going to be coming back. The house will be sold soon, and I'm afraid I'm just not well enough to travel anymore."

"Like ever?"

"Like ever."

"So do you think I could come there for a quick visit?"

"Define 'quick visit.'"

"A few days."

"Would you be coming by yourself?"

"Well . . . I would have come with my girlfriend, but she's not my girlfriend anymore. We broke up. She was really nice. Like you said, I found someone nice. She helped me move out of the motel, and she took really good care of me after my leg surgery. Her name was Clara." My voice cracks. I take a few deep breaths.

"What happened, Charlie?"

"I don't know. Lots of things went wrong. I was stuck in her house recovering from the accident. She started to find out too many things about me. Like how screwed-up my childhood was. Like how Mom abandoned me. And how my dad ran off with the babysitter. And how my little brother has grown up into a psychopath. It was just too much for her. She was nice, but it just didn't work, Mrs. M."

A pause. "Liam is a psychopath?" she repeats. "Please tell me you're exaggerating."

"No, he's trying to get revenge on me for leaving him with Dad."

She sighs. "Where does he live now that your dad has run off with the babysitter?"

"You won't believe this, Mrs. M. My mom actually came back to Grand Rapids. Liam lives with her now."

"Really? Hmmm. And so now the two of them are back in your life?"

"I've seen them, if you call that being back in my life. It was Clara's idea. She didn't know what she was getting into. And now Liam is driving me crazy. You wouldn't believe what he did when . . . ah never mind, enough about him."

"No, I'm genuinely relieved to hear he's not trapped with your father anymore."

"Whatever. So what if I came out to visit you for a few days? Would your sister be okay with that?"

"She won't mind. But you will be shocked at how I look. I was Miss America when you last saw me, compared to how I look now."

"Did you lose your hair again?"

"Did you ever see the movie *E.T.*?"

"Ouch. Do you want me to help you find a red wig?"

"I don't think I could pull off red anymore. I'm warning

you, Charlie. You won't recognize me."

"I promise not to scream when I first see you."

A wheezy sound. She is laughing. Hearing her laugh makes me laugh. We both laugh for a few blissful moments. Then she says, serious again, "I'm afraid I have a condition. Before I will allow you to visit me."

"Hmmm . . . where have I heard that one before?"

"You're not going to like it this time either. If you want to make a road trip out to visit me in Iowa, I don't think you should come alone."

"I can't bring Clara. I told you, it's over."

"I was thinking of that brother of yours. The psychopath. I'd like to finally meet him, Charlie."

"That's not possible."

"Oh, I think it's probably possible. Might not be easy, but life is hard, as you and I well know."

"He won't do it, Mrs. M."

"Are you sure? I'll bet you could find a way to get him to come. Now that he's back in your life."

"I don't *want* him to come."

"Then I'll just have to die without seeing you. That would be very sad, wouldn't it, Charlie?"

"Jesus!" I exclaimed. "You haven't changed."

"Neither have you. Take it or leave it."

◆ ◆ ◆

Clara has come home from work without saying hello, and now she is warming a can of soup for herself in the kitchen without asking me if I am hungry. I come close and stand behind her, waiting for her to acknowledge my existence. She slowly and deliberately puts down the spoon she is stirring the soup with and turns to me with the most impatient expression. "What is it, Charlie?"

"I called Mrs. M. today," I tell her. "We had a good talk, and I've made a decision. I'm going to take a trip. To Iowa. To see her one last time. And as soon as I get back, I'll move my stuff out of here, okay?"

Telling her this seems to deeply affect her. She looks up into my eyes, and I see that she is suddenly holding back tears. "I think that's a very good idea, Charlie. If it would help, you can borrow my car for your trip to Iowa."

"Really?" I hadn't yet given a thought to how I would actually get to Cedar Rapids. "But wait, Clara. How would you get back and forth to work?"

"I'll work it out. I have Monday off next week—I would only need to take the bus two days if you promise to be back by Wednesday."

I nod, figuring out times and distances in my head. "Today is Thursday. I could leave early Sunday and be back late Wednesday night. But, Clara, there's one more little detail I should tell you. Mrs. M. has a certain requirement for my visit. She is very manipulative, have I ever mentioned that? Very, very manipulative."

"Just tell me the requirement, Charlie."

"She says I have to bring Liam."

"Bring Liam?" Clara echoes. "Why does she want you to bring Liam? Does she even know him?"

"Actually she's never met him."

This surprises her equally. "In all the years you knew her she never once met your brother?"

"Never."

"Even when you lived with her?"

"Especially not then. I was pretending I didn't have any relatives except her."

"And she let you do that? Pretend you didn't have a brother?"

I am about to tell her that I can't explain it, but I stop myself. I can explain it.

I take a deep breath and confess, "Actually, Mrs. M. worried about Liam from the beginning, but I always told her he was doing fine even when he wasn't. When she found out that Dad was sleeping with the babysitter, she made me write a letter to Mom about it before she would let me move in with her. And not too long after that, Mom came back to Grand Rapids. But I never told Liam any of this. He thinks Mrs. M. didn't care about him any more than I did. Not true. I just didn't want to share her. I still don't want to share her. But I called her today, and she said 'Take it or leave it.'"

Clara is frowning, taking it all in. Her hair is windblown from the car, half out of her barrette, curlier than usual around her face. *You're so beautiful*, I think sadly. She paces for a moment, then goes back to the stove, turns off the burner, and asks, "Charlie, what makes you think Liam would agree to go on a trip with you?"

"I've been thinking," I tell her. "I thought about it all afternoon, see, and I've decided that if *you* asked him to go with me, like as a favor, he would probably say yes. Especially if he thinks that I don't know you're asking him."

Clara tips her head in utter bewilderment. "What are you *saying*?"

"I know, I know. It's a strange request, given all the things

I said . . . before. But I really need to see Mrs. M. It might be my last chance. And Liam would never say yes to me. He needs to think that it's another way to get back at me."

"I don't understand. Would you be there? When I ask him if he'll go on a trip with you?"

"I would like to be there," I admit. "But I have a feeling it will work better if I'm not there."

Clara crosses her arms tightly across her chest and sticks out her chin. Her voice is quavering but unusually loud. "Jesus, Charlie—why is this idea okay with you now? Suddenly you don't care if I'm alone with Liam? Why don't you care? Is it because you're over me already?"

I don't know how to answer. It seems pointless to respond. What difference does it make how I feel about her? I will never get over her. I say, "Clara, I need to see my friend before she dies. Please help me. Please talk to Liam."

This makes her put her face into her little hands and break down.

I stand awkwardly, my arms stiff at my sides, wondering if it would even be appropriate to comfort her, to hold her, when she surprises me by bolting across the space between us, wrapping her arms tightly around me and laying her damp cheek against my shirt. "Okay," she says. "Okay, I'll help you this one more time."

I hug her back for a long moment, then whisper, "Do you have his phone number?" Forgetting that of course she has it. And he has hers.

"I'll call him tonight, Charlie. I'll arrange to meet him somewhere. Starbucks or something."

I nod, resting my chin at the top of her head, inhaling the

scent of her hair like a starving man. "Don't tell him we're breaking up," I say. "It'll go better if he doesn't know."

Clara nods against my chest, agreeing to my sad request. Apparently, I am very persuasive when I am pathetic. Guess it runs in the family.

TWENTY-THREE

"Charles!" she gasps. I am standing at the stoop of her second-floor apartment—a ten-unit brick building on a quiet street in East Grand Rapids. It's a nice neighborhood, tree-lined and shady, houses on either side of the apartment complex, lots of porches. Her front door is painted sky blue with a cursive Welcome sign above the peephole. She is really surprised to see me. She says, unnecessarily, "I wasn't expecting you."

"Probably not."

"How did you get here? Is Clara—"

"It's just me. I can drive now. I take the boot off while I'm driving, and then put it back on when I get out of the car."

"Oh. That sounds good. Is anything wrong?"

"I just needed to tell you a few things. One thing in particular. Something that's come up with me and Liam."

"All right, then. All right. Come into the kitchen. Excuse the mess. Liam is already packing for school." Her voice is shaky. I have unhinged her, coming over unannounced like this. She puts a hand on her chest as she leads me to the kitchen, as though to protect her heart. I want to tell her to calm down. I want to tell her that it's not such a big deal that I have come.

But I suppose it is.

Even in the kitchen, there are the signs of serious packing—stacks of books on the far side of the table, boxes filled with music paraphernalia, and near a sliding door leading to a small balcony, yes, three suitcases. Matching new suitcases. Khaki with black trim, very masculine. They instantly infuriate me. Mom sees me staring at them and says, "A going-away present from his music teacher."

"Is that where Liam is now?" I ask, although I know perfectly well where Liam is now. I had recently dropped Clara off a block from the café where they had arranged to meet.

"He did have a lesson earlier," Mom says. "But I don't know where he is now. He's usually home before this." She looks faintly anxious.

"What, Mom?" I ask. "Are you worried because you haven't seen him in a few hours?"

This finds its mark. She receives the blow mournfully, then looks past me, to the small apartment balcony where a single lawn chair sits, as though longing to be alone there. I remind myself that my reason for being here was not to upset her. I make my voice more conversational and continue. "Actually, I came over to talk to you about—"

But something stops me. Something sitting atop a stack of Liam's sheet music on the kitchen table stops me. A single copy of *Meet Beetle Boy*. The first one. The one that came most directly from her own voice into my ear. Our eyes light on it together. It completely disorients me, this proof of what we did to her stories.

She seems also to be having a hard time deciding what to say. She does not look at me directly, but she brushes the book with her fingertips and murmurs, "I asked Liam to leave one here for me."

"Did Liam ever tell you how much we hated those books, Mom?"

She sighs. "Many times. He threw the rest of them away."

Not quite. The next words rush out of me. "God, it makes me sick to think you actually have one of them. I never wanted you to see what we did. I couldn't stop him, Mom. He kept wanting to take it farther and farther. He wouldn't give up. He wouldn't let it die. We were so trapped." I put a hand over my mouth to stop the final words: *How could you leave us?*

She says in the same soft voice, "I know. I always thought . . . I used to hope . . ." She shakes her head and finishes plaintively, "They were such silly stories, weren't they? To end up hurting you both so much."

I am calm again. My voice is cold. "Then why would you want to keep a copy, Mom?"

She grimaces. "I don't know. It seemed that I should have just one. To remind me."

"Remind you of what?"

She crosses her arms over her chest and waves one hand at the wrist, a pleading gesture. Her face is collapsing, and I am more than happy to change the subject back to why I am there. "Never mind. Never mind. Like I was saying before, I'm here because I wanted to tell you about something that Liam and I are planning to do together. Something he might not have told you about yet."

"You and Liam . . . together?" Now she is confused.

"Yeah, because you know that older woman I was living with when you first came back to Grand Rapids? The one who moved away?"

"I always wished I could have thanked her. For helping you."

"Well, there is a way that you can thank her, if you still want to. Because she's very sick and she wants me to come to Iowa and visit her. You know . . . one last time."

"Oh, dear. Is it that serious, Charles?"

"It is."

"Oh, I'm so sorry to hear that, oh, dear. Let me . . ." She moves to the cupboard beside her stove and takes down the blue teapot. It pains me to see it. I want to tell her that I don't like tea, but I remember that Dad used to make fun of her for drinking tea instead of coffee. I hear his voice, in the room with us, teasing and belittling her: "Miss Lucinda and her special tea." Remembering this makes me glad that now she can have tea whenever she wants. I let her make some for me, observing that the ritual—water, kettle, tea ball, and spoon—seems to calm her. Then I get back to business.

"Liam has decided to come with me to Iowa," I say with great certainty.

This throws her, I can tell. She pours the tea, a cup for both of us. "But Liam leaves for school in less than two weeks, Charles."

"I know that," I say. "We'll be back in time. We're leaving Sunday, and we'll only be gone a few days."

"This Sunday?" She is clasping her cup for dear life. She does not like this idea. These are her precious final days with Liam before he goes away. We are both silent a moment, sipping, refocusing. Then she says, "I'm just so surprised, Charles. Liam hasn't mentioned anything about going on a trip with you. Although," she admits, "he doesn't tell me everything."

I bite my tongue.

"And I can certainly see why you would want him to come with you."

"Can you?" I ask, curious. "Why do you think I want him to come with me?"

"As a way for you two to become . . . more like brothers. Before he goes away." She adds, nodding hopefully, "Maybe it will be a journey of healing."

She looks at me as she says this, stops nodding, and looks me straight in the eye. "A journey of healing," she repeats somberly. Then asks, "Is there some way I can help you, Charles? Do you need money for your trip?" And I think, *Mission accomplished.*

◆ ◆ ◆

With cash in my pocket, I drive back to the street corner closest to the café, where Clara had told me she would be waiting after one hour. She is standing under a streetlight, and when she sees me driving her car, she waves to me, but the gesture is a bit defeated. I wonder if Liam might have stood her up. But when she gets into the car, she says, "You were wrong about me convincing him, Charlie. He wants to talk to you. He wants you to call him tonight."

"Did he at least seem interested?"

"I would say yes. But he also seemed worried about leaving your mom. He said they had planned to do some things together before he moved up north. Since he won't be coming home to see her on the weekends."

Then she is quiet, and I wonder if she is considering offering to go with me to Iowa if Liam won't go. An offer I would definitely say no to. It would be a mercy trip, and she has shown me enough mercy.

"Mom will let him come," I say. I am sad, realizing that any sort of trip with Clara is now impossible. We never got to hit the road as a couple. We never really went anywhere together. Most of the time I couldn't get off the sofa without her help. It was a pretty miserable excuse for a romance, such as it was.

Clara asks finally, "Charlie, if Liam does agree to go, will you promise me that you won't let him drive my car?"

"You don't think he would be a good driver?"

"There's just something about him. He's so jittery. Does he have ADD? Has he always been like that?"

A sigh escapes me. "I won't let him drive."

"And one more thing. Right before I left him at the café, he asked me if I knew about your dad and Ruby. I acted like I didn't know anything, and he told me I should ask you. But I'm not going to ask. I'm just telling you that Liam brought it up."

"Clara, Ruby was the babysitter who—"

"Had a thing with your dad, I figured that much. Seriously, I don't want to know. I think it's just another way that Liam is trying to . . . make you look bad. Make things harder for you. Like when he was calling me. And when he brought your mom to the restaurant."

And when he broke into your house, I add silently.

She sighs wearily. "I just hope you two don't kill each other on the way to Cedar Rapids. When are you going to call him?"

"I'll call him right now."

Clara leaves to run a bath, probably needing to wash away the muck of the Porter men.

Liam picks up immediately.

"It's Charlie," I say.

"Okay, wait just a minute."

I hear the sound of a sliding door. The balcony. I can picture him sitting on the deck chair in the darkness with his cell phone.

"Clara says you're looking for a road buddy," he drawls. "She was practically begging me. I don't get it. Why don't you just take her?"

"She has to work," I say. Then, being more honest, "Mrs. M. wants me to bring you."

"Yeah, that's a good one," he scoffs. "Since when does she give a rip about me?"

"Since the beginning, Liam."

"Quit lying, Charlie."

"Not lying. She asked about you, pretty much from day one." I pause and then, "She gave me food for you. She asked me to bring you to her house. Like dozens of times. She told me not to forget you. But I didn't listen. Obviously."

There is a long silence. I would have thought that Liam had hung up on me were it not for the crickets chirping in the parking lot under the balcony. Finally, Liam echoes, "Obviously."

Another cricket chorus.

Liam asks, "So us going on a road trip deal wasn't your idea?"

"No."

"Clara made it sound like it was your idea."

"Look, Liam, I know it's a strange request all around. But this woman saved me. The same way that your music teacher saved you."

"My music teacher? I never said Mrs. Davis saved me. She gave me a violin, true. She gave me free lessons, true. She helped me get into Interlochen, true. But she didn't *save* me. I saved myself. Once I told Mom I would live with her, I saved her too. She's a different person now. She's happy."

I was fresh from my earlier conversation with Mom, and I pictured her frowning face, her trembling hands. It occurred to me that maybe there is something about me that makes her crumble. Is it because I am the son who was already gone when she came back? The one who made his own solitary escape? The one whose forgiveness she hasn't earned?

Liam interrupts these thoughts. "So suppose I agree to go with you to meet this woman who—now you tell me—gave a rip about me; that would take time away from my last two weeks with Mom, right?"

"I'm aware of that."

"Then there's something I need you to do. In exchange."

I brace myself for whatever he is about to require.

"You need to start visiting her after I leave for Interlochen. Take her to lunch. She likes going out for lunch because then she doesn't have to drive in the dark. Twice a month would be good. Do we have a deal?"

"I don't even know if she'd want that, Liam. I make her really nervous, haven't you noticed?"

"Just bring Clara. Everything goes better with Clara."

I ignore this and let my thoughts linger on the earlier part about Liam knowing what Mom likes. Is he the only person on earth who still knows this? No wonder he's worried about leaving her.

"Okay, Liam," I agree. "Twice a month. Even if she hates it."

"And we'll for sure come back on Wednesday?"

"We have to. Clara needs her car back."

"She's letting you take her *car*? Awesome! We can take

turns driving. I have a learner's permit, but I never get a chance to drive on highways."

I keep quiet on this one.

"You need some money for the trip? I can ask Mom. She has a little more money now from an aunt who died. But she said after I leave for school, she might look for a job."

Impossible to imagine. "Seriously? Doing what?"

"I don't know. She said she wants to work with kids."

Work with *kids*? Is there no end to the irony of my life?

"She gives me anything I ask for," Liam says. He is gloating now. "She basically can't say no to me."

I tell him that I have the cost of the trip covered. If he finds out it's because Mom already gave me money, so much the better. "Come over to Clara's on Sunday at nine." I tell him. "Don't be late."

"Wish Clara was going with us," he says, and I cannot mistake his implication. Just a few days ago, this would have made me hang up on him in a rage. But at the moment, it strikes me as so flamingly immature, and also so transparent, that rueful laughing ensues.

Liam hears me snorting with laughter. "What's so funny?"

"Don't you get it, Liam? We're still fighting over the babysitter. We're like a couple of little kids—'like me the best, like me the best!' It's so stupid, Liam! You've got to start seeing how fucking stupid it is. Or else neither one of us will ever have a chance at a real girlfriend."

"I don't know what you're talking about," Liam grumbles. "You have a real girlfriend, and I can have one any time I want."

I let him have the last word. At least, for once in my life, I gave him some brotherly advice.

TWENTY-FOUR

Clara turns out to be an absolutely expert packer for road trips, apparently from dozens of road trips all over the United States with Don and Susan. On Saturday afternoon she gets out a large and a small cooler, two coffee thermoses, a GPS device, maps of Illinois and Iowa, several different emergency kits (are we climbing mountains?), a travel bingo game (are we twelve?), a stack of magazines, and a bag full of energy bars and fruit cups. All of this is piled onto her kitchen table.

"You have to stop this, Clara," I say. "You have to get control of yourself. I'm not leaving the country."

"I know," she says. Then admits, "I can't stop. I have to help you."

Her mother calls every few hours, hoping to talk her daughter out of letting two unreliable misfits take her car out of state.

"They don't understand," she explains. "They think you're trying to use me."

"I am using you. But I swear I'll find a way to pay you back."

Late in the afternoon, Don comes over and tunes up Clara's car, giving me many looks of scorn because I don't know the first thing about tuning up a car—I'm a bike man, remember? Before he leaves, he says, "Time to get a move on, son. Time to stop taking advantage of people who are too nice to kick you out the door."

"Clara did kick me out the door, actually," I remind him. "I'll be moving into my own apartment when I come back." I say this as though it will happen easily, all planned, although I have no idea where I will be living. One thing at a time.

"You and your brother better just be damn careful with this car. No monkey business."

"I'll be very careful, Mr. Morrison. Thank you so much for taking a look at it before we go."

I don't know why I am even conversing with him; he so clearly doesn't like me. Maybe it's an old persistence— ingratiating myself with people who tell me to get lost. As scowling Don drives away in his truck, I feel a wave of happiness that I will soon see Mrs. M. again, the original "get lost" person in my life. Perhaps I will hug her; I never hugged her good-bye. My old friend. And I am not stressed about sharing her with Liam anymore. What difference does it make? Now that he is going away. Now that I am going away. Now that she lives far away.

◆ ◆ ◆

Then it is Saturday night, and we are packing up the car. It is a new experience for me, but Clara is very good at it—knowing which items to keep close at hand and which to put in the trunk.

"Charlie, does Martha Manning even know you guys are coming tomorrow?"

"I told her it would be soon," I say. "I'll call her in the morning and tell her we'll be there before dark."

"Aren't you even a little worried that Liam won't come over when he's supposed to?"

"He'll come," I insist.

"I want to hear all about it. Will you call me from the road?"

I am about to remind her that I don't have a cell phone, when I remember that Liam has one. "Sure," I tell her. "I'll let you know how everything goes."

"You seem so calm. I've never seen you this calm before."

I take a chance that she is feeling fondness toward me, and I touch her hair, cupping the side of her head. I am wondering if she might let me sleep in her bed for old time's sake before my departure. I am wondering if she will let me kiss her.

She grimaces sadly and says, "Charlie, please. Don't."

But she doesn't kick me off the couch. We watch TV together for another hour, and then she helps me unfold my bed. She goes into her room alone. I stay up a little longer with the TV off, staring at the walls, saying good-bye to Clara's house.

◆ ◆ ◆

We are all going to Iowa, the four of us leaving in the darkness, like escapees, taking a rowboat instead of a car. I am nervous, but both Clara and Lucinda insist that it's safer if we travel by boat. Lucinda is wearing her Mary Poppins sweater. Clara is wearing her lab coat. Her bright red hair is in two stiff braids. Liam is a child, dressed like a pirate, running around on the pier and waving a wooden sword.

I notice that there is a large cardboard box in the boat's hull. A box of books. Beetle Boy books. I protest to Clara and Lucinda that Mrs. M. doesn't want my books; nobody wants my books. But Lucinda says something was needed for the front of the boat for balance because something heavy is missing.

"What is missing?" I ask, but I already know.

Clara has begun to cry softly. She says through her tears, "He finally just crawled under my bed and died. I'll have to clean up the mess when we get back."

I tell her she doesn't have to clean up the mess. I promise to do it. I beg her, "Don't do anything else for me."

Clara says, "I can't stop myself."

Lucinda says, "We had a big one in our apartment too. Liam stabbed it with his sword." She looks at him; he is fidgeting around in the boat, oblivious to the rest of us, and she adds, "There is something wrong with your brother."

"Stop talking," I tell them. They are upsetting me, and I need to focus on getting us to Iowa. I need to row. I see that there is only one set of oars.

Clara is digging into her purse for something. She pulls out a map of the midwestern states, our path in red—Michigan, Indiana, Illinois, and Iowa. There is a photograph of Mrs. M., an inset on the map's border, and I recognize the photo—it is the same photo that was on the back cover of all the Franklin Firefly books, Mrs. M. in a fake, bookish pose, looking up from a still-blank sheet of paper at her antique desk. Her face changes; she is smiling at me. I see she is holding the diamond pen.

"Clara will be our navigator," Lucinda says. But she sounds afraid. I am afraid too. Afraid of getting lost, even with the map, even with Clara. Liam cries out, "I want to row! Let me row!"

I awake with a start and hear Clara, talking in her bedroom. I can hear from the strange timbre of her voice that she is dreaming too. I get up to look at her, make sure she is okay.

She rolls from one side to her other side as I watch her settle back into sleep. She murmurs, "Can I help whoever is next?"

TWENTY-FIVE

In the morning, as planned, I call Mrs. M. I wait until the last minute, because it is an hour earlier in Iowa, and I remember that she wakes up slowly. Her sister answers on the third ring.

"Why are you taking so long?" Helen demands. "I need someone to help me right now."

She sounds so urgent. I am startled. "Well . . . I'm coming tonight," I say, "with my brother. She said I should bring him."

"What?" she exclaims. She is near tears. "Who is this?"

"It's Charlie Porter. I'm Martha's friend. She knows we're coming. We won't stay at your house. We have—"

"Oh. Oh. I'm afraid I have some very bad news for you. I thought you were the funeral home director. Martha died in her sleep last night. I found her this morning. I'm sorry. I can't tie up the phone right now."

"No wait, no wait—I talked to her last week. She said—"

"She's dead, Charlie. So there is no reason for you to come."

My mind is spinning. I can't find my voice. I manage to

croak, "Won't there be a funeral?"

"She did not want a funeral. There will be no funeral. I really have to go."

"But wait, but wait—did she say anything about me? Anything I should know?" Her past words of advice were flying through my head: *find a nice girl, be a fifth-grader, make some friends, bring your brother.*

"There were no last words. No good-byes. It's very hard. I'm so sorry to have to tell you." She was choking up. "I have to go now. Someone is here."

She hangs up. I am still holding the phone, but I have fallen to my knees. The room is shrinking. Someone is howling uncontrollably from the end of a long tunnel.

Clara hears from the curb and comes running in. I cover my head with my arms, not wanting her to see this, my unbearable disappointment. "What happened?" she exclaims, coming closer. Then she says, "Oh God. She died, didn't she? She died before you could see her. Oh, Charlie. Liam and your mom are here! What should I tell them? I don't know what to tell them! Oh no! She died!"

I put my fists in my eyes, and the howling resumes.

"Charlie, they can hear you!" She hurries to the front door to tell them why I am freaking out. I hear her voice through the breaths between my sobs. She starts speaking matter-of-factly but soon becomes hysterical. "Because Charlie is upset. Charlie is very, very UPSET."

Liam comes bounding in. Mom stays frozen at the front door. She looks like she is about to die herself. Her face is as pale as I have ever seen it. Her hand is at her heart, fingers splayed. Liam comes right up to me. He puts a hand on my shoulder. His voice is oddly cheerful. "Hey, hey there, Charlie-boy. Hey, now. Come on. It's not so bad. It's not the end of the world. She was old. She was sick. Am I right?"

I say through my tears, "You idiot. You fucking idiot, you don't know."

"Hey, we can even go somewhere else if you want. Right, Clara? Right, Mom? Here, get up and come on over to the couch and take a load off."

His words jolt me from my grief. They stun me. My brother is being a good Porter man, digging deep into our shared past. I wipe my tears with both hands and look at him. I manage to say, "God, Liam. You have no idea how this feels." But then I realize that of course he does. He does know. He's forgotten, but he knows.

"Hey, I'm just saying we can go somewhere else." He is actually smiling his dazzling Porter smile. "I'll drive. Not a problem! Back on Wednesday! Let's do it!"

I see him so clearly then, all his damage, his resemblance to our dad, despite his time of healing and ascending. It's as though Dad is suddenly in the room with us, talking Charlie-boy and Leemster out of their motherless pain. Liam is upset, and he is trying to help me in the only way he knows how. I look past him, and there she, is our mother, standing in the doorway. She shakes her head at me slowly, and I think maybe she is disagreeing with Liam's advice—don't take a load off! Don't go! But I am not sure. Not sure that she can handle this any better now than how she handled things back then. I do not know her well enough to be sure; that is the chasm between us. Clara is standing beside her with one arm around Lucinda's narrow shoulders. Lucinda she can help. She does not know how to help me. I can see in her face how excruciating this is for her. I have distressed them so deeply, each of them, with my display of uncontrolled grief. But my mind grasps at something, and I think, *At least none of us are children anymore.*

I wipe my face with the back of my hands. I get up from my knees. It is very difficult. My leg is still weak. I move to all fours and then stumble and lurch to a full stand. Then I say, gruffly, "I think I need to go somewhere by myself, okay?"

I move past them, through the front door, avoiding their arms, ignoring their calls. Then I am in Clara's car, and I am driving across the city. I know where to go. The car seems to be driving itself.

I end up at her house. It's the closest I can get to her today. There is an addition to her For Sale sign. The word *SOLD.*

◆ ◆ ◆

I recognize him from my hazy memories of someone helping me while I was thrashing in the street only a few months ago. Mr. Carter. He must have seen me sitting in my old chair on the front porch. I am not wearing my walking boot; I came unencumbered. He waves, smiling. If he notices I have been crying, he doesn't mention it. He says, "How are you there, Chris? Remember me? Glad to see your leg is okay. Are you here about the desk?"

The desk. The desk is still inside. I had forgotten all about it.

"Martha mentioned that you might need some help with it."

"Right," I say. Then admit, "Actually, I have no idea what to do with a desk like that."

"You can get a good price for it. I know a thing or two

about antiques. Martha asked me to advise you. I mean, if you want my advice."

"Oh, I do. I really, really need some advice today."

"I have a friend who's a dealer, and he more or less specializes in antique desks. I could give him a call."

"That would be great. I can pay you if he buys it."

"Oh no, I'm happy to help Martha. I got a nice commission on her house. What do you hear from her lately?"

"Not very much," I say.

"Where are you living these days? With your gram so far away?"

"I don't have a place to live actually. I was living with my girlfriend, but we broke up."

"That's too bad."

"I know."

"Well, you can't live here anymore. The new owner is coming in a week. A family of four. Two little boys."

"They'll love it," I say. My voice thickens. "It was the best place I ever lived."

He looks at me for a long moment, scratching his whiskered chin. Perhaps he is just now noticing my disheveled state, my red eyes. He says hesitantly, "You know, son, I have an empty room at the back of my house if you need a place to stay for a month or two. I mean, since you're Martha's grandson."

I am suddenly holding my breath. I say, "I can pay the rent. I have a little money from my mom."

"Martha's daughter?"

I shook my head. "She didn't have any kids. I was her... honorary grandson."

"*Honorary* grandson? Is that right? Maybe that's why I feel like I can trust you not to make any trouble in my house."

"I'll be too busy to make trouble. I need to find a job right away."

"Do you want to see the room, Chris? There's a small bed in it. And a dresser. And a chair."

"That sounds fine. Did you say it's in the basement?"

"No, it's at the back of the first floor. With a separate entrance."

I find that I am faintly disappointed. But quickly recover. First floor is good. Bed is good. Separate entrance is good. Aloud I say, "Thank you so very much, Mr. Carter."

"You can call me Frank."

"Okay, Frank. I'll come later on today with my stuff. A few things. Some small boxes. No furniture. And I promise I won't stay long."

"All right then. And I'll call my friend about the desk. You can tell Martha I'm helping you."

I agree. I do not want to tell him yet that Mrs. M. is dead, in case that makes him change his mind about me. Too unconnected now. Too alone. Just me and a few boxes and a walking boot and one gigantic desk.

I get up from the porch chair and limp over to Clara's perfectly packed car. Time to go back and face the three of them; they will be waiting for whatever I will tell them about my next move. I will be standing on both legs when I tell them. They will see that for once I am sure about what is best for me.

Before I start the car, I lower my head over the wheel and whisper, "Wait, wait, since when am I sure about what is best for me? How is anybody ever sure about that?"

My questions echo in the empty car. I have no idea what I am doing. But there is no terror in my uncertainty. I actually feel pretty strong, stronger than I would have ever thought possible after such a terrible morning. Strong enough to get through the rest of this day, definitely.

At least the story that comes now will be all my own story.

I take a deep breath. I start the car.

I think I got this, Mrs. M.

About the Author

MARGARET WILLEY has writen in many genres over a career that spans decades. All of her books and stories come from a personal place, either something that happened to her or something she witnessed at close range. *Booklist* called her most recent novel, *Four Secrets*, "rich in unique voices" in its starred review. Margaret lives in Grand Haven, Michigan, with her husband, Richard Joanisse. Visit her online at www.margaretwilley.com.